D1506535

The Candidate's Wife

Also by Virginia Coffman
in Thorndike Large Print

Dark Winds
The Orchid Tree

This Large Print Book carries the
Seal of Approval of N.A.V.H.

The Candidate's Wife

Virginia Coffman

THORNDIKE ~ MAGNA

Thorndike, Maine U.S.A.
North Yorkshire, England

Library of Congress Cataloging in Publication Data:
Coffman, Virginia.
    The candidate's wife / Virginia Coffman.
        p.   cm.
    ISBN 1-56054-255-1 (alk. paper : lg. print)
    1. Large type books. I. Title.
[PS3553.O415C36   1992]   91-29409
813'.54—dc20   CIP

British Library Cataloging in Publication Data:

A catalogue record for this book is available from the
British Library.

ISBN 0-75050-132-4

Thorndike Press Large Print edition published in 1992
by arrangement with Severn House Publishers, Ltd.

Cover design by James B. Murray.

The tree indicium is a trademark of Thorndike Press.

This book is printed on acid-free, high opacity paper.

The Candidate's Wife

- ONE -

Afterward there were as many reasons as there were witnesses to what had happened. But, of course, it had been a long time in the making.

Senator Jessica March spent the night before her party luncheon speech in a hotel suite in the city, but it hadn't done much to relieve her tension. She awoke early on a morning unusually warm and sultry for summertime in San Francisco. Even before she opened her eyes, she recognized the now-familiar stomach-tightening nervous tension that gripped her before every political appearance.

She was thinking: Is this what Chris will want me to say? Would he answer the question this way? Of course! He checks most of my speeches beforehand anyway. What am I but his carbon copy, his way of holding down two national political spots at once?

Jessica was an old hand at worrying, and once she began, the other thoughts came along faithfully like the caboose that followed the loaded train. But a new and treacherous little thought came unbidden that morning of her San Francisco speech, and the real twisting and knotting began throughout her body.

Suppose, sometime, I don't *want* to say what Chris would say? Ridiculous! Ex-Senator Christopher March's opinions are sacred to his wife. Why else did he manipulate me into his senatorial seat when he was named to the cabinet? Yes, but suppose, some day, I have an idea of my own. Suppose —

Stop it! Just stop it!

She lay there trying to follow her own advice, repeating to herself the opening of her luncheon speech. The first time it went off well and with a certain spontaneity, but for some reason, her mind blanked out tiredly on the second attempt. Panic began to creep over her body. Stimulated to activity by the tightening of the nerves between her shoulder blades, she rolled the covers back and sat up. After a long deep breath that momentarily relieved the tension, she put one foot experimentally over the side of the bed feeling for the smooth, yet prickling touch of her apricot satin mules.

I've accomplished one thing with this entire nervous-indigestion bit, she thought. If it is indigestion, at least, it keeps me thin. She got some satisfaction in studying her neat foot: No calluses or corns there — ever. Chris still boasted he had fallen in love with her ankles and her feet. If he were with friends, as opposed to constituents, he might add that her legs had something to do with it too.

She had been seventeen years old and a part-time theater cashier when he met her. He wasn't much higher on the financial scale himself, though his position couldn't have mattered less to the romantic and impressionable Jessica who had grown up on a diet of dashing, sexy males on the screen of the neighborhood movie house her mother managed.

The box office was glass, and the way Jessica Souza sat on her high-backed stool in front of the ticket vending machine had been of the utmost importance. Skirts had been long and full in 1951, but by crossing her legs correctly, young Jess could reveal "by accident" a very fetching length of nylon just a fraction above the knee, but no higher. The rest of that slim but rounded body might be — and often was — guessed at from this teaser displayed.

Eighteen years and two teen-aged children later, Jessica found life with Christopher March even more exciting than she had ever imagined it would be but not quite as romantic as it ought to be. While her feet slipped into the dated, but specially made satin mules, she called down to the hotel message service.

"This is Senator March. May I have my messages now? . . . Yes, but I seldom sleep after seven. Habit, I'm afraid."

There were half a dozen requests for interviews from Bay Area newspapers who had known her since the year one, or so it seemed, and a Washington, D.C., columnist with a gift for malice "wanted to check a rumor." That last would inevitably be a rumor about Chris and some Capital hostess, one of those ugly needle-pricks as painful to feel as to deny.

"No messages from the children?" One would think seventeen-year-old Robin, in his first year at Berkeley across the Bay, might at least squeeze out a phone call when his mother was so near. But she snapped out of that mood. He had been unavailable when she called him last night and was probably "playing it cool."

It had been Chris's idea that Robin live near the campus, where Chris himself had gone to college. Now the boy was madly involved in strikes, picketing, and even spent a night in the city jail, along with all the other accoutrements of a "higher education." Chris was furious, feeling this tarnished the responsible-liberal image that, as a presidential hopeful, he was carefully nurturing. Jessica found herself in the middle of this schism and, like most middle-roaders, was resented by both sides.

"I'm sorry, senator," said the young feminine voice over the phone. "We don't seem to have any calls from Mister Robin or your daughter. But," she added cautiously, sensing that this was bad news, "there's somebody who just stuck his head in here. He says," she giggled pleasantly, "he's your secret lover. Shall I give out the news to those columnists in the lobby? What a scandal that would be, huh?"

Jessica stiffened with the shock of delight. Chris had flown in from Washington to surprise her. And it had been years since he joked about being her secret lover.

Secret Lover! It must be Chris!

She told the hotel's message service to send up a bellman with the messages so she could take care of the newsmen, and then asked to be transferred to Room Service. She ordered two continental breakfasts.

"And what kind of jam is it this morning?" she added on a sudden thought.

"The *confitures*, madame? Strawberry and apple. Are they satisfactory?"

She looked down at her feet in the satin mules and smiled with a memory: "Do you have any apricot jam?"

Fortunately the jam for tomorrow was to be apricot. Senator Jessica March was promised all the apricot jam she could desire. This time she laughed, and in that moment's happiness the heartburn in her breast — it had risen from her stomach — seemed to relax and leave her tense body at peace.

11

"Not for me, for the senator," she caught herself. It was still a mistake she made upon occasion. "I mean — the ex-senator. He adores apricot."

We had it on our wedding morning . . . when Chris suddenly produced that wholly unexpected thousand dollars for us to sail to Hawaii and back. Rates were cheaper in 1951!

And Chris would never tell where he had gotten that thousand dollars, though he had been so worried about living on his salary as checker for a theater chain. She need never worry about that; Chris had acquired the money honestly. Even in those days he was much too ambitious politically to do anything dishonest, anything that might hit back at him.

She slipped out of bed, shrugged into the double layer of nylon and net that matched her nightgown, and hurried into the bathroom to wash, shower, and make up. But she had gotten no further than washing when the hall door buzzer cut noisily into the air and she started to rush through the foyer to greet Chris. At the last second she managed to recover a precarious dignity as she opened the door.

"Good Lord, darling! You should have let me know and I'd have sent a car to the air —"

She felt pretty foolish to be talking with such enthusiasm to her husband's severest newspaper critic, "Bick" Haldean. She had known Bick, of the virile reputation and excitingly hard face, longer than she had known her husband. Bick had worked his way through the University of California as a ticket-taker and occasional bouncer in the theater managed by Jessica's mother.

He was standing there now, looking her up and down with his bold hazel eyes that had a kind of humorous crinkle about them, and she almost expected him to pick up where he left off, in the old movie-house days, by offering one of his kidding-on-the-square propositions.

"Hello, gorgeous. That is," he amended, cutting her off as she opened her mouth, "*senator* Gorgeous. You act as if you didn't expect me."

"You know damned — perfectly well I didn't expect you! What the devil do you want at this hour? It's barely dawn."

He tried to look hurt, but she had always suspected that if she ever did hurt him, he wouldn't let her guess it.

"You told them downstairs to send me up. Well," he spread his arms wide, "here I am, ready to go to work." The work he had in mind, she was amused to note, seemed plainly sensual. He was sidestepping toward her bedroom and the unmade bed.

She was never entirely sure when Bick was really on the make. It was a game they had played occasionally over the years. She wondered suddenly, with a slight but not unpleasant flutter of self-consciousness, whether Bick remembered the late spring night, just before she met Chris March, when she had discovered sex, mistaking it for love. Parked in the Oakland Hills, in all the comfort and roominess of a prewar station wagon, Jessica had taken Bick's undergraduate course in the art of love. But whether from a sudden lack of interest, or an uncharacteristic desire to save her honor Bick had returned her to her mother's apartment technically still a virgin. Was he thinking of that now? She rather hoped he was. The knowledge would do much to make up for the disappointment of seeing rugged Bick Haldean when she had hoped to see her husband's always thrilling features instead.

But there would have been something more important than just her pleasure at seeing Chris? she thought. His arrival now and in this way might affirm her hungry hope that he cared more for Jessica, his wife, than for Senator Jessica, his political doppleganger! On the other hand, it might have affirmed the opposite! This gave her such a painful twinge that Bick clutched her bare arm and shook her slightly.

"What is it? Jess! Are you all right?"

He hadn't called her Jess in eighteen years, and she was warmed by his unthinking reversion to the pleasant days of their youth.

"I'm perfectly all right. It's this nervous indigestion I kgeep getting." She smiled up into his face. He seemed extraordinarily concerned and the knowledge touched her. "I'm trying my best to start an ulcer, but the pain always goes away."

"What you're doing is the hardest kind of work. What the devil are you campaigning for when you ought to be off somewhere, taking it easy, cruising or living it up? I didn't think you were that ambitious, *senator*."

She was trapped into the angry admission: "*I hate it!* I hate the speeches and the awful questions and the heckling from Juan Alvaro's union hoodlums, and the constant worry that I might say something he —" she broke off abruptly. She had been goaded into a betrayal she had never made before, even to her own children.

"Go on," he said with a grimness that surprised her.

"Nothing. You know perfectly well we shouldn't be talking like this, especially with me practically naked. What a juicy bit that would be for someone's column!"

"Honey, it wouldn't be the first time I've

seen those stunning bones of yours. Tell me the truth. I've always suspected it. When McClatchey appointed you to fill out March's term, it wasn't to satisfy any blazing ambition of yours, of course. We all knew that. But there was some sort of finagling going on. Isn't Secretary of the Interior good enough for March? Is it the Department of State he's after? How can it help him for you to be a California senator?"

She stepped into the closet, got out a heavy satin robe of floor length and put it on, knotting the cords at the waist with nervous fingers she could hardly control. She heard Bick's exclamation before she saw him.

"Good God! Don't tell me. Mister Kleen wants to be vice-president of the United States!"

To avoid the real problem she said crossly, "Don't call him Mister Kleen! You know he hates that . . . and so do I."

"Come here into this sumptuous living room. Might as well use it, long as you've paid for it."

"I haven't paid for it. I get the whole suite for the price of the bedroom, and Sue Lyburg, my secretary, is just down the hall. Anyway, I'm expecting breakfast any minute, and if you're seen here —"

"Don't be silly! I'm interviewing you. Come

and sit down. God! I hate these Louis Fourteenth chairs! It's like sitting on a slippery turtle's back."

"Louis Fifteenth," she corrected, but she smiled as she joined him. It was good to be on friendly, even intimate, terms with Bick again after all the years of his biting attacks on her husband, his passion for the braceros, the grape-pickers, and the Mexican-American minority whose cause was usually espoused only through political expediency. She knew Bick's passion for justice was sincere. He was always shooting his mouth off — which cost him jobs. But worse, he was extremely articulate with a typewriter, and he never could understand how a man like Christopher March, who had once defended the cause of both Mexican nationals and Mexican-Americans in California, could turn against them during his two terms in the Senate. Explain as the Marches would, Bick never quite believed that March still loved his early constituents and only hated "their political leaders."

Bick couldn't be made to understand that radicals had gotten hold of these long-suffering field workers under the guise of unionizing, that Bick's labor-leader hero, Juan Alvaro, was very likely a communist. Chris had told her often enough. It was becoming a litany with him by now. But people like Bick were blind; they simply refused to see the truth.

"Bick," she began firmly, attempting to serve, as always, in her husband's best interests. Somehow her enjoyment of Bick's very male company made her feel guilty, and she felt the least she could do was to straighten Bick out about Chris March's position. "My husband has been the best friend the braceros ever had. And as for the other Mexicans —"

"Who are United States citizens," he cut in.

"Well, naturally! But you yourself know they've had no chance for a decent education. Some of them can't even read. Chris has put through two bills to help them. But meanwhile, this Alvaro acts like their savior. All this talk about unions and strength of numbers is just to get these poor devils into his power!"

Bick grinned, but she thought his eyes were not amused. "How true! And only our Mister Kleen is equipped to take the good, simple, childish people under his wing. Jess, hon, why does everyone assume that uneducated people are ignorant people?"

She had just sat down, but she got up again in a hurry. "Oh, Bick! Go try out your next column on someone else. I've got a headache and a stomach ache and my chest hurts. And you sit there jabbering silly aphorisms!"

He took her thin hands and although she was angry, she was unbelievably tired. She let him draw her closer.

"Jess, you are quite a woman. Is this really you, the sweet, skinny kid with the good legs and the nice little cashier's job, spilling out words like *aphorism* and talking so condescendingly about people like your Portuguese father? Did you know there's even talk that Alvaro may be assassinated? He's got some mighty sticky enemies."

She burned to answer him, to deny that she was condescending, or that anyone would be so stupid as to kill his beloved Alvaro, but some of the wind was taken out of her sails by the sudden interruption of the buzzer, and she exclaimed in a sudden panic, "I ordered breakfast for two. I thought you were Chris. It's going to look bad, your being here. It's as if —"

"Brazen it out," he advised her. "Don't, for God's sake, act guilty!"

"Why should I? I'm not guilty of anything — certainly not anything of with you."

"I am."

She looked at him.

"But only in my thoughts," he added, with that teasing look she used to think of as both humorous and sexy.

Nevertheless, she was shaking inwardly

when she crossed the suite to the foyer door, not because she was afraid of the bellman's lascivious thoughts, but because this was just another little problem to worry about. What with the children's antagonism toward their father and Chris's terribly driving need — his dream — of being nominated vice-president to run with the incumbent, President Walters, this was no time for the future vice-president's wife to be caught in even a hint of a "breakfast with an old boyfriend." The one watchphrase that had guided her married life for eighteen years swept over her: What would Chris say?

Still, it was too late to worry over that now. Chris would really laugh if he knew the conversation that went on at this romantic breakfast, such as Bick's preposterous suspicion that someone might murder his precious union organizer, Juan Alvaro. Mr. Alvaro probably spread the rumor himself; it would certainly gain him the sympathy of the do-gooders and bleeding hearts.

Jessica opened the hall door more carefully this time, being cool, indifferent and, as Bick had suggested, anything but guilty.

"Thank you. Bring it in there. An interviewer is here now, and I need my coffee before I can take care of any more hecklers."

The young bellman grinned back at her as he rattled the tea wagon over the doorsill.

"Sure thing, senator. You get 'em full up on breakfast and they're easier to handle."

"Hold it! Nice work, senator," called a lean collegiate-type fellow behind the bellman. He was spinning off pictures of Jessica as fast as the little flash cube would snap around. As she blinked, he raised the cheap but obviously efficient camera over the bellman's head and snapped what Jessica knew must be a compromising shot of Bick Haldean close behind Jessica who was in her satin dressing gown.

The curious thing was, she realized that she cared very little. The pain behind her breastbone had started again . . . so many worries . . . it was hard to concentrate on just one.

– TWO –

While the waiter set out the two breakfast trays on the cocktail table in the living room, Bick remarked, to Jessica's surprise, "I hope you've got no problem with coffee nerves, Senator March." She stared at him and belatedly understood as he continued in a loud voice, "It isn't easy to have coffee with Bill Royd and the *Chronicle*'s McChesney and the rest of the gaggle waiting for you."

"Oh — those? Yes," she began vaguely. Then she caught the drift of his remark and perked up noticeably as she saw the retreating photographer stop and frown before leaving the doorway. She was happy to see that Bick's remark about her other breakfast companions disappointed him; he felt the scandal nature of his pictures had been diluted.

When she turned around and got a really good look at Bick, putting on his little act of note-taking for the benefit of the waiter, she found it so ridiculous of him, she almost ruined his act by laughing. Making an effort at control, she said severely, "I'm afraid I'll have to ask you to limit your questions, Mr. Haldean. As you remind me, I do have a number of appointments. I'm sorry."

She was sure the waiter lingered in the foyer. Probably he got his cut for any news or gossip he could relay to the press.

Bick peeled off layers of a buttery, flaky croissant and with an eye on the foyer, ate while he questioned Jessica. He used that loud, carrying voice for the benefit of eavesdroppers.

"Now then, senator, ma'am, is it true you're sponsoring a move to investigate the citizenship of Juan Enrique Alvaro, the union organizer?"

"I know who Mr. Alvaro is, Mr. Haldean. To answer your question, I am not personally sponsoring any investigation. However, if this man is here illegally —"

"He isn't, ma'am."

"Yes . . . well . . . at any rate, if he did lie to obtain his citizenship and someone has found out, I see no reason why he should be above the law."

Bick took a long gulp of coffee and began to stride slowly toward the foyer. As he passed her, he gave her a quick but careful glance. She had a feeling that her answer, her frankness about that troublemaking unionizer had disappointed him, and when he left her now, she was no longer "Jess, hon" but once more her husband's dutiful shadow, Senator March.

The hall door closed gently as Bick neared the foyer. Jessica, hoping to mend matters now that they were alone, said with genuine warmth, "It was good talking to you, Bick, after much too long." She held out her hand, but he didn't seem to see it. He was looking rather deliberately at the hall door.

"Sure," he agreed. "Sure. Tell you what . . . never mind. See you around."

She hadn't time even to walk through the foyer with him before he had the hall door open and was looking back.

She said, "I'd better change if I'm going to entertain the patient press."

For a brief moment he was the man who had called her "Jess" and "hon" half an hour ago: "No. Don't! Stay as you are." He laughed, human and friendly again. "If you are seen in that satin thing with half a dozen reporters, nobody can accuse you of conduct unbecoming to a U.S. Senator. Safety in numbers, remember."

"Thanks, Bick. I'll remember." She was at the door now and rested her cheek against the door panel as she watched him leave. For a few seconds she had a terrible premonition that he would not turn around, that their long antagonism since her marriage was about to be resumed.

Finally, though, he did look back. He

didn't grin this time. His eyes were hooded, unreadable. "You look mighty sexy standing there, senator."

Then he turned the corner into the big, red-carpeted general corridor leading to the elevators and was gone from her sight. She burned pleasantly at this comment, thinking how nice it would be to just remain warm and calm and easy like this, the way it was in the early days when Robin and Bethy were little, when her problems were the all-encompassing problems of a wife and a mother.

Those were the days, she thought with a sigh, and went back into the suite to call downstairs for her next visitor. Each visitor meant that she must constantly be on her mettle, looking for cuts, darts, and barbs that might cause her to give an answer that reflected badly on Chris.

How good she had felt during most of that hour with Bick! She had almost forgotten how exciting and virile he could be. Nerves and small problems had a way of dissolving in his presence — even if he didn't agree with her over people like that Alvaro troublemaker. If only Bick could appreciate Chris's position on such things! It was people like Bick who had caused the split between Chris and the children. Being young, they were inclined to side with an outsider, rather than their own father.

Two hours later she was still repeating to the last of the reporters, "My husband is a true liberal. His entire record in the Senate demonstrates his liberal views."

The ancient question of his civil rights stand made her bristle defensively: "His civil rights record speaks for itself. Everyone knows the great driving passion of his senatorial career has been to better the condition of the Mexican-Americans in California and the Southwest. My own father, Jaime Souza, worked in the vineyards when he first came to California."

She was surprised to see her last questioner, a clever young woman from Stanford University, jot something down in a little bright-green notebook with lilac pages which Jessica recognized came from Takahashi's. A notebook from the enchanting Japanese shop was amusing to her because she wrote all her own speech notes on such gayly colored pages; she found they cheered her up enormously.

Watching the girl write and then whip the notebook back into her well-filled and tailored pants, Jessica asked curiously, "Hadn't you known my father was Portuguese?"

"Sure, senator. I just jotted down your hair color. You're awfully light for a Portuguese."

This is what they mean when they talk about being "taken aback," Jessica decided and managed to explain dryly, "Only my hairdresser knows for sure." But it was annoying. She had always been proud of her sandy gold hair which, at the age of thirty-five, still required nothing more than a heightening rinse.

The question of her children's involvement in politics being indirectly against their father's stand came up, as it had with the other reporters, and she gave her stock answer that she and Chris were proud of the independent thinking of Robin and Bethy. But the question always bothered her. She knew, as she hoped these questioners did not know, that Bethy and Chris were growing more embittered against each other every day.

Anyway the girl was gone at last, and Jessica hurried to shower and dress for her luncheon appearance. So much had happened since she awoke with the now-all-too-familiar chest pain that she hardly noticed the troublesome and intermittent pain now. Pelting her body with the sharp shower spray and then following this with a self-inflicted rubdown, and a vigorous massaging with a good friction lotion, she felt infinitely better than she had when she awoke several hours earlier.

She still had vague, prickling worries about having said something today that Chris March's enemies could use. There were so many things to remember, when even the color of her hair might have political implications. Somebody could always accuse her of trying to hide her Portuguese origin by dying her hair. So far, nobody had accused her of hiding her Irish mother's blood. Something she had long suspected Chris's mother would prefer to forget.

Unfortunately, Augusta March also could not forget that when her son had needed a shadow-senator, someone to hold the California Delegation for him to pressure the president at the convention in late August, he had chosen his wife instead of his politically trained mother who had been a committeewoman for twenty years — and a national committeewoman during the last three elections. There were many moments, particularly when Jessica was suffering from what she called "frantic nerves" that she herself would gladly have voted to be replaced by her ambitious mother-in-law.

Jessica's correspondence secretary, Sue Lyburg, bubbly and young, borrowed from Chris's staff, was still untrained enough to oversleep, came barging in to interrupt Jessica without knocking, and then chatter for ten minutes about a party in Berkeley last night with the Young Californian Marchers for March.

"And the cutest go-gos, Mrs. Jess! All rooting for your husband. It's too groovy! Just grabs you to think of so much he-flesh at one party. I nearly went out of gig!"

"Was Robin there?" She knew he wasn't but hoped against hope that Sue would surprise her.

Young Sue shrugged with a consciously sexy rotation. "You know Old Impossible! He got a call from his — from your daughter, Bethy. Something about that Mexican organizer. That's their bag. She and Robin simply don't know *darling* Senator March the way I do. It's often the case with parents and children."

Jessica looked startled, and Sue added hastily, "Your husband, I mean. I think it's awful the way his own children are so against him. Are you feeling all right, Mrs. Jess? You're looking kind of pale." Jessica glanced into the dressing room mirror, and the girl went on catching Jessica's eyes in the reflection: "You look great with those wonderful cat's eyes. They're really shaped like cat's eyes. Oh! I didn't mean — no, really! Everybody says you're the best-looking senator in either party."

Jessica grinned ruefully. "Thanks a whole lot. You forget, I've seen the rest of the Senate." However, the girl was right, she did look pale. She got out blushers, dark contour foundation, and powder and redid her face. It seemed, perhaps to her imagination, that she had aged several years since the day eight months ago

29

when Chris and Dexter Dominik, his campaign manager, maneuvered Governor McClatchey into appointing her to fill out Chris's senate term. From the first she had dreaded and even hated it, but there was no question about the help her job gave to Chris politically. He had never been able to count solely on Governor Simeon McClatchey, tall, husky, only just going slightly gray, but a stupid man and too easily maneuvered by others just as Chris maneuvered him.

"I wonder if I have time to call Bethy. Sue, would you —"

"I'm awfully sorry, Mrs. Jess, but we really are a little late. You know how Mr. Dominik gets."

Jessica shivered and set the perky silk cap with the stiff little peak over one eye. "Don't mention that man's name to me. He makes my flesh crawl."

Sue Lyburg picked up Jessica's handbag, gave a proprietary pat to the collar of Jessica's bright Pucci dress, and followed her out, protesting, "What? That smooth D.D.? You know, Mrs. Jess, those colors look so flattering on you. Nobody'd better criticize it, that's all."

They reached the elevator before Jessica gave in to her bitter, driving uncertainty.

"And why would anybody want to criticize it?"

Flustered, Sue stammered, "I only m-meant . . . because it's so high-styled. Those awful old battle-axes at the luncheons! You know."

"Too well. Here's the elevator. Do you have any of those indigestion things?"

"Another stomach ache, Mrs. Jess? I have a couple of your Donatols."

"No, I have a Gelusil in my bag." She hated taking prescription drugs. She was always afraid she would begin to rely on them too much. She chewed up two Gelusils in a hurry, and for the moment they seemed to help. At any rate, she felt more confident when they reached the plush lobby, and then the curious phenomenon began again. All eyes seemed directed her way, not in flattery but with a kind of inhuman curiosity.

When she saw elegant Dexter Dominik make his way through the suddenly silent lobby hangers-on, with those teeth of his flashing like beacons in the sun-lamp brown of his face, Jessica had to think of something else, and quickly. To her husband's eternal annoyance, she had taken what amounted to a revulsion toward his favorite political campaigner who was a born infighter.

Jessica said quickly, "Sue, would you mind calling Bethy's school? If she isn't there, try and talk to one of her friends. See if we can't get a phone number where I can reach her."

"Still the little mother," remarked Dexter Dominik unctuously. "I don't think you need trouble right now about Bethany, Miss Lyburg. I doubt if she can hurt Chris, with her little shenanigans." He took Jessica's arm in a grip surprisingly strong for such a smooth-skinned, unblemished hand, and, as usual, she found it impossible to avoid him.

She did get in the cutting reminder: "I'm not interested in whether or not our daughter is hurting my husband's image; I want to make sure she is safe and well and happy! Sue!"

The girl's eyes darted quickly in D.D.'s direction, then back to her boss, impressed by Jessica's sharp summons. "Yes, ma'am. Right away. I'll use the public phone over by the ballroom."

The thing that pleased Jessica most was the way D.D., as Chris called their Frankenstein, realized his place, that he had been interfering in the private life of the Marches.

After this little victory of Motherhood over Politics, Jessica hated to come under and acknowledge D.D.'s superiority even in his own field, but she managed to ask with brisk competence, "What is first on the agenda?" And then, because she couldn't resist the question, "Have you heard from Chris lately?" That last word suggested embarrassing and painful inadequacies in her own contacts with her husband in Washington, and she corrected herself hastily, "That is, this morning?"

Dominik shot off names as if reading them from an invisible cuff. There were a dozen women whose names Jessica tried hard to remember, wishing her memory for trivia was better developed.

"Mrs. Capp is the Homemakers' March . . . Mrs. Pudney-Clormann of Croisetti Farms . . . Mrs. Duvaux is the Vintner Marchers' president. All three are useful when Chris moves on."

"Moves on from vice-president?" she asked, surprising herself by the sarcasm in her voice.

"Precisely. Miss Catarina San Felice, aged seventy-plus, will be along today too, another Marcher for March — and the vineyards she represents could keep you and me, and Chris too, in diamonds for several lifetimes. You simply must fit the names to the faces. Ah, here she is. The charming Gladys Duvaux. And how is our beautiful Queen of the Grape-growers today?" Not for nothing had D.D. learned his trade as a lobbyist in Sacramento!

The Queen of the Grape-growers had gushed up to Jessica as she and D.D. passed through the crowd of chattering women in the Gold Room Bar on their way to the Gold Ballroom which was to be the scene of the luncheon. Jessica, who remembered how important the Duvauxs were in one of California's leading industries, tried to be especially friendly, and when the woman, in an obvious brunette wig reached out with a half-spilled glass of wine in her hand, Jessica mentally connected the hand with the wine woman.

Mrs. Duvaux, her handsome eyes sparkling, suggested, "You will have one teeny drinkie, won't you, Madame Senator? Just to show you're one of us."

Misreading the "us," and still seeing that hand with the outstretched cocktail, Jessica reacted with enthusiasm: "Perhaps I will. A martini, please — with a twist of lemon." The bartender took her order but already, from the tension which surrounded her suddenly, Jessica knew she had made a mistake.

Mrs. Duvaux caught her breath as if she had been slapped, somebody nearby laughed, and, worst of all, Dexter Dominik jabbed Jessica in the ribs with his elbow. He too laughed, but playfully.

"You can see, Jessica's sense of humor has been underestimated." Dominik looked around at the barman. "Make that a Duvaux wine fizz."

Everyone joined in the laughter, including a slightly hysterical outburst by Jessica. The ghastly undiplomatic error was glossed over. It was only then that she realized how many wine-growers were represented here in the oak-lined, masculine-looking bar, by wives, daughters, and sisters of the men involved in the vital grape culture. Small wonder, she thought, that Chris stood so firmly against Juan Alvaro. For nearly a hundred years migratory workers had been employed seasonally, both in the grape country north of San Francisco and in the fields of the once-arid desert of the San Joaquin. Such migrants considered themselves fortunate to be making five times the two-dollars-per-day salary they would be making in Mexico. And though the pay they made in California was not guaranteed, or year round, they certainly would be foolish to antagonize their paymasters by unionizing. Yes, Chris *must* be right.

She wondered why the nagging little question occurred to her at all, except, perhaps, that the sour wine fizz only riled her stomach up more than ever. She wished suddenly that Bick Haldean was here close beside her in D.D.'s place. And then, as the impact of that forbidden thought hit her, she closed her eyes momentarily. Dominik shook her arm. Someone had asked her a question which she failed to answer.

"Strike?" echoed Mrs. Duvaux, "Don't be silly! What good would a strike do? Only one-tenth of Alvaro's riffraff are unionized."

"That man is a menace!" cried another woman shrilly. "I'd give a thousand dollars if somebody'd just take a pot shot . . . well, what I mean is, if we never had to deal with that man again, we'd all be happier."

"Ladies," suggested Dexter Dominik, with one of his eyebrows arched significantly, "perhaps a change of subject would be in order?"

Whoever had been making the rash financial offers lowered her voice. Other conversations began to take over but, quite close, Jessica thought a man's voice murmured, "Perhaps a raise in the ante. Maybe you can outbid the job." This was followed by D.D.'s familiar laugh.

A woman cut into this odd remark so loudly that Jessica was not sure she really heard it at all. "Madame Senator! I've been dying to ask: do you ever have rows with dear Senator March — I mean Senator Christopher March — about politics, or anything?"

"Since Senator Christopher March has always been right — in my eyes — I couldn't very well argue any points with him," she said sweetly. But to herself, and for some perverse reason, she added silently, was that remark as phoney as it sounded to me? Did I really agree with Chris this morning when Bick was talking to me so passionately about his beloved migrant workers?

Dexter Dominik put in his little soothing addition: "We all know that Senator March would not be here in this room with us now if she were not being a dutiful, loving wife. Don't we?"

There were quick-voiced agreements. Jessica wondered what would happen if she herself, having, of course, gone absolutely insane, suddenly bellowed out: *No! We don't!* This morning I spent a beautiful hour in a sheer nightgown, entertaining an old boyfriend.

But she did not say it. She wasn't quite that insane, and, she told herself sternly, she wouldn't have meant it anyway.

– THREE –

Somebody in the crowd had again mentioned the possible strike of vineyard-workers and Jessica caught only the end of a curious remark: ". . . justified, I'd say! Like our right to bear arms!"

There was an eery little silence that lasted barely ten seconds, as if the overheard and indiscreet words found a horrible echo among the listeners in the cocktail lounge. But it was so sudden and so complete it shook Jessica out of her concern with that tiresome burning in her chest. She would have to take the Donatol after all. Would nothing stop this persistent indigestion?

"Sue?" she called, swinging around. "Do you have those pills handy?"

The girl was making a fairly successful play for Dexter Dominik's attention, a sight that Jessica hated to interrupt. Anything to keep his mind, his all-seeing eyes, and his enormous polished teeth away from her! Sue handed the small white pills across a pair of intervening Marching with March members who were busy arguing something that would cost between three and four thousand dollars.

Jessica asked, "Sue? Did you get a number where we can reach Bethy?"

"No. I'm sorry. Her roommate said Bethy got the Tiburon businessmen's ferry this morning. Nobody's seen her since."

"Oh, Lord! Where on earth can she be?"

While Jessica swallowed the pills with the aid of a gulp of wine — against doctor's orders — she tried to be polite and politic as well, listening to the senseless conversations of those around her, while her real thoughts were with her daughter's odd behavior.

". . . It'd be worth it," said someone. "My husband says they always assassinate the wrong people. Nobody's caused more misery and discontent than —"

"My God! Be careful, Puddles. I'd rather not know. I'd really rather not. Anyway the whole thing's in good hands. Let's talk about something else."

"Good hands? Murder? I mean . . . well, what else would you call it but —"

There was another voice in the confusion of the room, a man surely: "It is called eliminating the competition, I believe, ladies."

Giggles drowned out anything else. Jessica looked around. What weird bits and pieces of conversation one heard in the noisy privacy of a cocktail lounge! If it weren't so incredible, it would sound like a murder plot. I've got to stop reading those mystery thrillers, she decided. I'm beginning to imagine things. "What time is it, Dexter?"

D.D., who had been flirting diplomatically with a stout little dark woman in a mink jacket, glanced at his wrist watch. "Another ten minutes. Anything the matter?"

"No, nothing. Just something I ate." She grinned feebly. "Or something I'm about to eat." She glanced around, took a couple of long breaths, and then, quite suddenly, caught a glimpse of a thin, searching, well-loved sixteen-year-old face in the doorway across the room. She waved joyfully. "Bethy! Over here!"

The leggy blonde girl in what was either a white pleated miniskirt or an old-fashioned tennis dress, waved a long, very slender arm, then hesitated on the brink of plunging into the ocean of women. Jessica gently but very firmly pushed her way between chattering groups toward Bethany March, reflecting as she did so that the blonde girl had a scrubbed innocent look which seemed at wild variance with the heavily welded Halloween masks that seemed to crowd the room. When Jessica was almost within a fingertip's reach of her daughter, a stout man and a thin woman formed a quick barricade, chattering in Jessica's face and waving highball glasses. Wine fizz, undoubtedly! As usual, they managed to spill a few drops that would hopelessly stain the new Pucci dress Jessica had hoped would cheer her up.

"Mrs. March, do you think it's true what the *Chronicle* said this morning, that your husband — that is our own Chris March — is the president's choice for a running mate?" the man asked.

"I've no idea — nor, I'm sure, has my husband," she lied and tried to pass by the pair.

His wife clapped her gloved hands. "I don't mind saying it was the luckiest thing in the world, Vice-President Groves dying like that. I mean if he had to die, we'd loads rather he died before the election that way. Of course, we miss Chris March tending to our California affairs a way back in Washington, but he'll tell you what to do when you go this fall. Don't you worry, Mrs. March."

Jessica stiffened, yet wondered why. Everyone knew, including herself, that she was a mere extension of Chris, that any ideas, any legislation accomplished during her term would be credited to Chris. But because she had her own pride and at least a modicum of political sense to defend, she said briskly, "I am sure we all regret the passing of Vice-President Groves, he will be hard to replace. My husband and I leave all such matters in most-capable hands. The president will have the final word on his running mate, as he should have, but we do value your good opinion. My husband will be pleased that you approved of his work in the Senate."

That squelched them without stifling their pro-March spirit. She reached around them to hug Bethy who seemed unusually tense and stiff in her arms. They stepped back to get a little square of space to themselves near the plush lobby entrance of the cocktail lounge.

Bethy pulled away and looked at her mother, wincing, her big eyes troubled. "Mom, you look ghastly! Are you okay?"

She said impatiently, "Of course, I am. I just had a grisly fizz — a Duvaux fizz, that's all. Is my makeup on lopsided?"

"No, no." Bethy reached out her long thin arms, gave her mother a brisk little shake. "Honey, you're as pretty as ever — or you would be if you got enough sleep. You should be back at the Maryland place, not out here campaigning for a phantom candidate. Future vice-presidents don't get campaigned for. Don't you know that?"

"Hush! Good Lord, Bethy! We've got to be discreet — at least until the convention." She looked over her shoulder, saw the usual complement of eyes directed their way and was sure the ears were likewise busy. She lowered her voice: "I've just had a case of indigestion. You know how it is with me . . . it comes and goes." She laughed nervously. "If only I had an ulcer, it would be more chic — an in-disease, I guess you could call it. But *nervous stomach?* Nothing glamorous about that!" She added in a hurry, "Let's talk about something else. How have you been, dear? Have you talked with Robin?"

Bethy linked arms with her, seeing D.D. beckon to them over the heads of the roomful of Marchers for March.

"I really think I'll make something of that boy yet. He's going to picket those nice, early-California, richly simple houses where the vineyard-owners purr and guzzle and enjoy life while they refuse even to recognize the field union."

"Really, Bethy! You sound exactly like an old Odets rerun."

"Well, it's true! I feel so — so Joan of Arc-ish! The field union needs me."

"Come along and tell me about Robin. And incidentally, when the luncheon is over, tell me what's wrong with my speech."

Bethy went along with her very companionably, obviously pleased when the cocktail crowd parted for her and her mother. "All right, Mom. But tell me one thing: why do you always laugh and make fun of the things I say? Like today."

Jessica flashed her a genuine smile, feeling momentarily uplifted by her bright, ebullient presence. "I make fun of your mixed-up metaphors, not your sentiments."

"Now, who's sounding like the Late Late Show? Who's that with his back this way? Lovely shoulders. Halfback shoulders. Cal or Stanford, I wonder. Hope he thinks blondes have more fun."

Mentally Jessica had begun to repeat the key ideas of her speech and did not for a minute see who Bethy was talking about. When she did look, her heart gave an inexplicable jerk which she supposed must indicate surprise. Bick Haldean hadn't told her he would be here. He was looking at her with those hard, deep-set brown eyes bright, as they had been once or twice this morning during her "interview." It made her extraordinarily relieved, and even delighted, that he had not been angry with her after their lively talk.

"Good grief!" Bethy quoted Charlie Brown. "It's Bick Haldean! He's going to do a series on Juan Alvaro's life and struggles and all that. He was at the union meeting up in Napa last night."

"Bethany March! You mean to tell me you were up in Napa last night instead of where you should be, in school?"

"Don't be stuffy, Mom! You can be a very

44

modern mother when you try hard. Besides, from Marin County to Napa, we can drive it in ten minutes."

"Don't let me catch you trying to do it in ten minutes!"

"Well, fifteen, maybe twenty." Then Bethy added impishly, "Anyway, I promise faithfully not to let you catch me doing it."

Jessica felt a little better to think Bick Haldean was in on the unionizing business. Whatever her personal feelings for Bick, past or present, she would trust her children to his care before any other man in the world. Then, realizing the unconscious implication, she corrected the odd thought quickly, guiltily: any man but Chris, of course!

Bick headed across the room toward them, and Jessica tried to decide whether he came as a result of Bethy's waving fingers or had started of his own accord. Someone tapped her arm. She swung around, her nerves on a string, and that string in the tensile fingers of Dexter Dominik.

"Time, Madame Senator."

"Yes. I'll be with you. Bethy, come and sit by me. Prompt me when I forget."

D.D. tried to get between Jessica and her daughter with a pretense at gallantry, a remark about "escorting two beauties," but Bethy nudged him out of the way with

45

a trim-hipped swivel of her short skirt whose pleats flew out, to the whispered shock of women behind her.

"Bravo!" Jessica mouthed the word to her daughter and they neared the elegant rectangular Gold Ballroom with its Versailles look, its sky-high ceiling and mirrored panels. Long ago when Jessica was eleven, her parents had taken her across the Bay for a grand birthday celebration, and they had come to this hotel. They had not eaten dinner in the ballroom, of course; it had been unlighted, rented only for special occasions, none of which was Jessica Souza's birthday. But on their way back along the thick-piled corridor carpet, the happy three were greatly daring and peeked into the ballroom. The floor was freshly polished. Jessica and her father had danced down its length and back, but in the end, all three of them were politely asked to leave.

We aren't leaving now, Mama, Papa. If you could only see your Jess this minute . . .

Now, so many years later, nothing had changed very much about the Gold Ballroom except that the gorgeous crystal lusters were gone. The mirrors had been changed, the gold panels had been regilded, and today the room was crowded with long tables, a great deal of old-fashioned white napery, sparkling glassware, and the hotel's ever-impressive crested china. Already, the tables seemed to be filled with well-dressed women and a sprinkling of men, staring at Jess the doorway.

"All for you, Mom," whispered Bethy, after a low and sexy whistle.

Jessica had almost believed this, briefly, before the truth crept in to make her say in a cross, audible voice, "Not for me — for your father. I'm only acting as his shadow. You know that. My own opinions have nothing to do with it."

This, unfortunately, was overheard. Mrs. Duvaux tittered — or was it Mrs. Capp?

"Why, Mrs. March! You mean to tell us you disagree with our Senator Chris?"

"How do you disagree with him?" put in one of the men who had interviewed her earlier.

Bethy began to push. "Leave her alone, can't you? She's carrying out Daddy's legislation, everything the way he wants it, so why don't you just shut up?"

Bick Haldean had made his way to them in time to hear that last remark. He was grinning. "I'll be sure and quote your opinion of us."

"Do that!" said Bethy, her small, pointed chin tilting up defiantly, but she followed this by reaching out with such gladness, such enthusiasm, to grasp Bick's hand that Jessica became aware of a very strong feeling, at least in Bethy. It was startling and terribly disconcerting to Jessica who couldn't quite understand her own reaction.

Was it possible there was some feeling between thirty-six-year-old Bick and sixteen-year-old Bethy? Surely, Bick had the common decency not to become involved with a child Bethy's age! Jessica glanced at him now, trying to keep her eyes veiled by the lashes, and was relieved to note what she thought was merely a friendly, almost a fatherly cameraderie on his part. Bethany, though, was a different matter. There was hero worship in her expressive eyes — and something more, something sensuous about her full, moist lips that would alarm any mother.

In tribute to the guest of honor a tape recorder, concealed behind the greenery back of the long speakers' table, struck up the old Chris March campaign theme borrowed from "Marching Along Together," and everyone rose. The noise of sliding chairs, dropping handbags and rolling compacts almost drowned the music. All eyes focussed on Jessica which was always disconcerting, and she had to remind herself firmly that though they looked at her, they were really seeing Christopher March in their collective mind's-eye.

Smiling pleasantly, but not broadly ("Don't overdo it, darling," Chris always said.) Jessica crossed the threshold into the room that had so captivated the eleven-year-old girl a long time ago.

Without quite knowing how it happened, Jessica found herself being maneuvered to her chair at the speakers' table by Dexter Dominik, and when she looked around, Bick had taken her daughter to a table halfway across the room and then sat down beside her. Jessica waved and Bethany waggled her fingers and grinned in answer. She then looked up at her companion and remained in that state of adoration — or puppy love? — while Bick talked to her about something or other.

The chairwoman of the luncheon, who happened to be vice-president of the Marchers for March — both sexes — made a sotto voce remark close to Jessica's ear and then laughed. Jessica knew she should laugh but said apologetically, "I'm sorry. What did you say?" and heard D.D.'s angry exhaling of breath on her other side. She no longer cared. She had a headache and a funny feeling that something important had passed her by today, something she had only partially heard and understood.

"I said, senator, if that communist rabble-rouser could see us here, with all this food around us," Jessica looked down at the cups of canned fruit cocktail, "he'd say we were headed for another Russian Revolution."

Jessica smiled politely.

"And all I can say," the annoying voice went on, beating what, at this gathering, was a dead horse, "is that Juan Alvaro deserves whatever he gets. Although, to tell the truth, I don't really know the details . . . and I don't want to know them."

That's it! Jessica thought suddenly. That's what I didn't quite get. Somebody is going to assassinate that Alvaro person!

She was so shocked at her own thought, she began to rise from her chair. Someone called out her name. People looked at her oddly. Bick and Bethany were getting out of their chairs across the room.

Then the nagging pain in her breast began to spread like tongues of fire through her body. She tried to speak:

"Only . . . indigestion . . . Somebody — water . . ."

Bick had nearly reached the speakers' table when the pressure in her breast and her shoulders and stomach became unbearable. She knew at last it was not indigestion but her heart, as she swayed and stumbled back. She did not feel anything when she struck the floor. . . .

– FOUR –

"Heart attack" was not a diagnosis made for public consumption; too much was riding on Jessica's presence at the convention in a little over two months. Nevertheless, as with most whispers, the mere fact of the secrecy surrounding Senator Jessica's "nervous indigestion" and "exhaustion" magnified her heart attack of slight-to-medium severity into a massive stroke, complete mental breakdown, and paralysis.

Her children suffered more than Jessica did, since, most of the time in the hospital, she was unaware of what was happening. And afterward there was another thing about it: when she was out of the oxygen tent and all its appurtenances, Jessica March saw more of her family than she had seen of them since her husband's second senatorial victory.

"That was a close call," half a dozen physicians, surgeons and relatives hastened to warn her repeatedly, and in all cases, secretly. This was thought necessary in view of Jessica's euphoria after she began to recover. If she died, the disaster to the burgeoning image of Christopher March as the president's running mate, would be incalculable. Everyone would be sure to say, "Chris is in mourning. It would be indecent of him to accept the draft. And besides, he drove her to her death."

There were exceptions to this concern. Bethany, slapping the tilted hospital bed emphatically, said, "I'm personally delighted with the whole thing, Mom."

"Well, thanks a whole heap," Jessica remarked wryly as she opened her makeup case, preparing to make herself reasonably healthy for the waiting press.

"You know, Bethy," she remarked, having twice missed an even curve with her lip-liner, "I've heard of people having to play down a disease, but this is the first time I've ever, had to *pretend* I had been nervously exhausted."

Bethy's expressive face twisted a little. "Don't say it, Mother. It was so awful, seeing our Rock of Gibralter keel over like that! How's your arm?"

The black and blue arm on which Jessica had fallen when she collapsed in the ballroom looked almost as good as new, though one of the elbow bones was sore and, as her doctor remarked cheerfully, "probably would always give her a little trouble." At any rate, she held the arm out while Bethy examined it approvingly.

"Thin, but nice. There's a shape to it anyway. I wish my own shoulders looked as nice. I'm getting all fat and flabby where I stick out of a sleeveless shell."

Jessica was amused at that and was still laughing at her matchstick daughter complaining about being too fat when her son came in. Appealed to by both females, he was able to agree, with the wisdom of his seventeen years, that his mother did definitely look healthy, and his sister was not only fat, she was repulsively fat.

Bethy took little notice of this, but got even by reminding her mother, "Robin did what you asked, Mom. He got his hair cut . . . about one-twelfth of an inch!"

This was, figuratively, hitting below the belt, and tawny-haired Robin's blue eyes sparkled with injured innocence when he reminded Jessica, "I shaved off my mustache."

"Yeah, all two hairs and a half!" his irrepressible sister put in, and if she had not accidentally joggled the bed at that minute, reminding herself and Robin of their mother, a very familiar argument might have ensued.

Jessica's use of an eyeliner was slightly curtailed, but all this commotion was so like the old days before the family was scattered, that she could forgive almost any joggling.

"Is there a great deal of work piled up for

your father?" she asked them looking from one to the other, for their passionate involvement with political, social, and economic matters had put them in direct conflict with their father, and Jessica lived in dread of the day when they might come out openly against him in a campaign.

Robin shrugged. "You know Dad. Right now, he's downstairs in a waiting room, running the interview with the press. The one that's supposed to be your interview."

"Good! He's welcome to them. Frankly, I'd rather not see them at all." She laughed, a bit nervously. "Maybe he can persuade them all to leave."

Bethy, who had gone to the window and pulled the blind aside to look out, said dryly, "One of them won't leave without seeing you. I know that."

Jessica felt a slight jolt. Not my heart, she thought. Just the old memories. Aloud she asked casually, "Oh? And who's the persistent fellow?"

Robin scoffed before Bethy could speak. "Who else but Bethy's swinger? Bethy's Bick."

"You keep out of this, Rob!" His sister's golden coltish arms reached for him but he neatly avoided her, slipping around Jessica's bed and, as luck would have it, backing into his father who had opened the door a couple of seconds before and witnessed the brother-sister skirmish.

Seeing the handsome, kindly lineaments of her husband's face look suddenly frozen, Jessica winced. The nagging little nervousness began again, as before her heart attack, and she thought, they're going to start in by fighting. The first time we've all been together in months! Then she remembered the warning repeated, almost mimeographed, by her doctors: "Don't let yourself worry. If you do, you may hurt them as much as you hurt yourself."

She said calmly, "Morning, Chris. How did the press conference go?"

"Surprisingly well. They seem to be satisfied." He leaned across the bed and across her makeup case. When his face shadowed hers briefly and he kissed her on the lips softly, with the tenderness that had illuminated so many of her dreams lately, she was surprised at her own excitement, and wondered if her face showed the girlish flush, the passion she thought had been crushed and watered down long ago.

The children, upset by his unexpected arrival, exchanged quick nervous glances and stopped their squabble instantly. Jessica caught this indication of their father's effect on them and noted a minute later — a fact she found even more painful — Chris's effect on his children was such that they forgot immediately all their private quarrels and joined forces against their own father. Something would have to be done. It seemed to her that this was more important than all the press conferences, campaigns, and possible chances to be vice-president. She gave Robin what she hoped was a sharp and significant look, over Chris's graceful bowed head.

The boy avoided her glance, pretending not to understand, but during the little time that Chris and Jessica talked, Bethy must have had a softening influence on her brother because they were both good mannered, if not wildly affectionate to their father, when he turned his attention to them.

"You're looking better every time I see you, darling," Chris told his wife, patting her hands and then, as Jessica warmed to this compliment, he took her fingers and kissed them as he used to during those first months of their marriage, like the time he surprised her by producing the hundreds of dollars which enabled him to lease an apartment in an excellent neighborhood, furnish it, and thus present a perfect front to the Mayor's Committee looking for Councilmen of the Right Sort.

He looked the "right sort" to her now, with

the warm sincere blue eyes, the gentle romantic mouth that could be so firm when he was denouncing those demagogues who took advantage of his earliest constituents, the Mexican-American laborers in the fields. She remembered with pride how he had helped both the Mexicans, often dumped illegally into California, and the owners of those vast agricultural empires who needed cheap labor. The children and the rabble-rousers they listened to simply didn't understand their father. They couldn't know his sincerity as she did. He was tallish, trim, never let himself gain an unbecoming ounce. He possessed remarkable willpower about such things.

She found him looking up from her hands, his face close to hers. He looked no more than thirty, with scarcely a wrinkle — and certainly no gray hairs. "Handsome as a movie star," she heard many women say, publicly, as they talked of his sex appeal in her presence. Even among the nurses in the hospital she had heard this kind of talk. It was flattering to Jessica in many ways. After all, it was she whom he had chosen, whom he had married and lived with all these years.

"Jess, you did wonders for me before this — this *thing* came on. Dr. Talmadge has been tearing me up one side and down the other. He says it's all my fault. I shouldn't have worked you so hard."

She was so touched by this that, even though she recognized some truth to it, she felt his tender and solicitous admission cancelled out any of its truth.

"No, dear! I wanted to do it, to help any way I could. It was simply that I got so worried about doing things right. I am always afraid I'll say something wrong, make some kind of stupid slip."

Robin interrupted hotly: "You were great, Mother! You've always handled those vultures just great! You just tried to kill yourself to suit a bunch of crappy —"

Christopher cut in in his quiet way: "Your mother did the finest job of which she was capable. We all know that. And, darling, you aren't ever going to be pushed and over-worked like that again. We're going to see to it, aren't we, gang?"

"The Gang" had been Robin's childhood name for the family during their camping activities in the Sierras, or when, on Mother's Day, the three of them prepared their special — if starchy — feast for Jessica.

"We sure are!" Robin agreed and, just a fraction of time later, Bethy added her voice to the general enthusiasm. Jessica thought it was worth the entire heart attack just to live through this precious moment when Chris held out an arm, drew his daughter close, and offered his free hand to Robin. Robin, like Jessica herself, was quick to anger and as quick to forgive and forget. But Bethany was different. It often seemed to those who knew the girl that, in many ways, she was older and far more complex than her brother. Jessica wondered what was troubling her now. One of her "causes," no doubt.

"Is Mom supposed to talk to the reporters now?" Bethy asked, cutting into the loving family scene.

"She means her beloved Bick Haldean," Robin jeered with a grin. "He's been hanging around the hospital for days — nights, too — he says — to get an interview with Mother."

Jessica glanced at her husband. Chris's gentle mouth hardened to an unpleasant line again.

"The less we see of that radical, the better. That series he's begun about Alvaro — glorifying a communist —"

"Oh, Daddy!" Bethy began, but intercepting a pleading look from Jessica, she shrugged, muttered, "Everybody who disagrees with you is a commie," but then she shut up.

Jessica also felt a slight inclination to be irritated with her husband. She told herself she might have known there would be no jealousy in Chris, not sexual jealousy anyway. If he thought anything at all about Bick hanging around trying to see Jessica, he would assume there were political motives. But then, of course, there were Robin's reasonings:

"Battling Bick's old enough to be Bethy's father, but maybe he's got a daughter complex. Maybe —"

"Shut up! Just shut up!" That was Bethany, but neither her fury nor her mother's angry echo had such an effect as Chris March's razor sharp:

"That's a vulgar remark! It is disgusting! Is that the 'great truth' you learn at Sather Gate, to make filthy remarks about a child your sister's age?"

While this argument went on, Jessica, having failed to calm them, finished her makeup, set aside her case, and swore to herself that she would not be provoked into nervousness or worry. But remembering Bick's influence on the seventeen-year-old Jessica years ago, she took no real comfort now in the difference between her daughter's age and that of the virile and powerful Bick Haldean. Besides, he had an aura of heroism — this defending of troublesome Juan Alvaro — which made him look even better to romantic, impressionable girls like Bethany.

It was awkward that when someone knocked

on the door, the children were still wrangling, Chris was laying down the law to both of them, and at the same time the phone rang. Jessica answered it, relieved at the interruption that no word of hers had accomplished. Another knock on the door made her nudge Chris and point wordlessly in that direction while she answered the phone. She was not connecting mentally with the call. It seemed to her much more important to find out who was coming in to see her. It might be — yes, it was! — Bick Haldean, coming ostensibly to interview her but actually to hang around Bethany!

Surely, I'm not *jealous!* I couldn't be! I'm only thinking of Bethy, so young to be involved with him. That's all it is: not jealousy, just concern!

And here was a voice, Long Distance was babbling away on the phone, with static interference and bits and pieces of dialogue adding up to nothing while Bick said something to Chris who received him coolly but with his usual good manners. The long-distance operator babbled on, overtaken now by a male voice, also babbling, while Jessica saw her daughter's face light up, the young vulnerable eyes all starry . . .

One thing appeared certain. Bethany was in the throes of her first serious infatuation.

But — of all people — Bick! Jessica's own first love!

"Hello? Senator March? Do you hear me?" There were clicking noises in her ear. "I said: this is the White House. Herb Millvale. Yes, senator. How are you feeling? That's good. That old nervous exhaustion can really get you down. I say, senator, I'm calling for the president. He wants to say a few words." Self-conscious laughter followed this, at the White House end of the line. Jessica could imagine that Herb Millvale was talking while the president was within hearing. Poor Herb! He had two ulcers and admitted gloomily that he had a third one coming on in this impossible job as the president's secretary and chief flunky.

Before she was ready for it, the president's urbane, polished, Manhattan squire voice came over the line, making her teeth ache as always with the implications of his superiority. Sometimes it seemed to her that a little of this urbane superiority was rubbing off on Chris: the rationale that, "I believe in only what is right; therefore, whatever I believe in *must be right*." She could understand that. Lots of people were that way. But the superior accent always rubbed her the wrong way.

"Good morning, Mrs. March. You had your friends a bit concerned for you there for just a little while."

"T-thank you, Mr. President. It's good of you to call."

"Well now, Jessica — may I call you Jessica? — I'm very fond of your husband."

"Please do, Mr. President." All sounds in the hospital room had stopped miraculously when she uttered the title aloud. In spite of herself, she was flattered. Some small part of her thoughts was suddenly busy asking her: Did you ever think the President of the United States would be calling Jess Souza to wish her a speedy recovery? Then the doubt . . . or was that really the reason for the telephone call and the solicitude?

"Jessica, we are counting on Christopher this fall. We need him here." He chuckled in the theatrical but effective way that made him a smash on television. "Naturally you can imagine how your health enters into the picture. I mean to say, you must be perfectly well during the next three months. Anything else would reflect seriously on Christopher."

Bewildered she lied, "Of course. I understand. But I'm m-much better. I really am. I mean, a heart attack isn't the end of the world nowadays. My doctors call it mild to medium. Sort of like a steak: medium-rare, I guess." Out of the corner of her eyes Jessica saw her husband's tense alert body and was not surprised when he made significant motions either to coach her or to take over. Had she said something wrong already?

But the president was saying something in that pleasant manner of a person correcting without flatly contradicting a false statement. "Not quite, my dear. Christopher will explain to you. You mustn't mention that business about the heart. You may have had some slight heart murmur, true. But, according to all we've learned from your excellent team of doctors, you have been suffering primarily from nervous exhaustion."

"I see." The flatness of her reply surprised even Jessica.

"Does he want to talk with me?" Chris whispered. She shrugged. Chris looked with annoyance at their unwanted visitor, Bick Haldean, doubtless wondering how much he had put together out of all this conversation.

Bethy said something to Bick, keeping him busy, but it seemed to Jessica that the old-war-horse newspaperman had one ear for Bethy's chatter and another for what was clearly a crucial briefing of the Marches by the president himself.

The president's voice had sharpened ever so slightly.

"Now, do we understand each other?"

That was clear enough — almost a threat.

"Perfectly, sir. And I feel fine, just fine."

"That's my girl. I know Mrs. Walters joins me in wishing you all the best from here on in. You just get over that nervous business. You're a big girl now, and we need that husband of yours — need him badly. So you're very important to us all . . . not," he added as an afterthought, "that you aren't important to us for your own charming self."

She thanked him quickly, anxious to hand over the phone to Chris, knowing her husband wanted it to appear that the president's call was actually for him. But the president, with good wishes for Chris, hung up, leaving Jessica in the position of handing over an empty line.

Worst of all, Bick's deep-set, dark eyes had missed nothing of the maneuver. Using her wits, Jessica said at once, "Mr. Millvale asked you to call him back, Chris. Some business that he's handling for the president." As Chris looked uneasily in the columnist's direction she went on, "Meanwhile, the rest of us will try and give Mr. Haldean some kind of interview."

Taking the hint, Chris excused himself and left the room. She had no idea whether he would call Herb Millvale or not, but at least he could now fortify, for Bick's benefit, the picture of a close connection between Christopher March and the White House. As for Jessica herself, she let Robin help her out of bed, under the interested gaze of Bick Haldean whose expression flattered her no end. She was particularly glad she had been persuaded to wear the new, sheer, apricot colored get-well robe Chris had given her. It was very nice to be admired again, and by a man of Bick's sensuous masculine aura.

"Isn't he groovy, Mom?" Bethany put in with a rush of enthusiasm. "He's already done two absolutely dreamy columns on Juan Alvaro and the true background about the start of the field workers' union."

Jessica smiled, genuinely glad for her daughter, though she knew perfectly well that every word in Alvaro's favor made her own job as Chris's shadow-senator that much harder, since the March campaign was geared to run *against* the organizing of the workers. Then she remembered something, a silly trivial item she had thought of briefly when she woke up this morning.

"By the way, take care of your friend."

Bick looked at her puzzled, apparently not aware that she was joking, but Robin and Bethy assumed correctly that her light tone was not to be taken seriously.

"My friend?" Bick repeated, clearly not understanding.

Bethy wrinkled her nose. "Oh, Mom! Not one of your dreams again! Mother always has dreams. She gets enough plots out of her dreams so she ought to be able to write a play or something. What was it this time? You found yourself in the Black Hole of Calcutta?"

Embarrassed now, Jessica wished she hadn't mentioned the mixed-up dream at all, but Bick was obviously waiting to hear it, giving her general appearance, from head to foot, a flattering examination.

"Bethy's right. It was pointless," Jessica said. "Something about your friend Alvaro."

"Not my friend," Bick contradicted her coolly, "just good copy. What about him?"

"N-nothing. Just a silly dream, but it bothered me a little. I'm not at all sure about the details. Anyway . . . it was as if I was in some dark, cool place. I can't imagine where. There was a lot of noise, but I couldn't make it out. Except I seemed to hear a voice in my ear — I don't know where it came from — just a voice. And it said something about it not costing much, or being worth what it cost, to kill a man." She laughed abruptly, seeing them all stare at her and added with a note of apology, "Why I should have thought they were talking about your Juan Alvaro I can't imagine. I don't even remember precisely when I dreamed it. It was almost as if I just woke up with it in my head. You know how dreams are."

The silence that followed was broken within a few seconds by Robin's easy laugh. "Well, there you are: Mother and her dreams."

They all laughed, including Jessica.

Yet, it had seemed so real, at least for a little while this morning, as if it had actually happened.

– FIVE –

There was one remark more than all the others that made Jessica groan with the repetition of it: "Take it easy, Jess." "Take it easy, Mom." "Take it easy, Senator March." Only her mother-in-law, Augusta March, failed to say that, but, then, Augusta was in Pakistan on a fact-finding committee and, believing her son's own publicity, hadn't considered her daughter-in-law's illness serious enough to bring her scurrying back with the resultant awkward publicity.

Actually Jessica had never felt better. Chris remained in California to help her, and most of all to be with her, to resume the old normal life she was beginning to think of as abnormally beautiful because it was part of the magic past. The day she left the hospital, Chris himself drove the whole family home across the Bay. The children insisted on cutting school to carry her bags and get her settled in once more at the March home in the Oakland Hills.

They crossed over the Bay Bridge in Chris's respectable middle-class Oldsmobile just as the summer fog lifted, and the beauty of the waters scudding under the eternal wind made Jessica blink back sentimental tears. It was hard to believe a few weeks ago she had been on the verge of death and that except for luck, she might never have been able to enjoy this incomparable view today. She knew nothing negative of this sort would be in the minds of Robin and Bethany; they were much too young and too enchanted with their roles in life to believe in death. But had the thought occurred to Chris?

He remarked now to Jessica who shared the front seat with him, "Looks like the Bay put on its best bib and tucker just for your coming-out party."

She smiled. It was like Chris to use these old expressions. He had found, on his first campaign, that the things he learned at Grandma's knee went over big with his constituents, even when they didn't understand anything he said. Often, when his expressions like "bib and tucker" were translated into Spanish, they turned into ancient Mexican sayings and made "Cristoforo March" sound more down to earth than ever.

Robin called from the back seat, "This interview you gave out at the hospital, it reads great, Mother."

"Yeah, great," muttered Bethy. "Nothing that could upset anybody."

Jessica kept looking scrupulously ahead. With great care she concentrated on the approach of the Yerba Buena tunnel, hoping the children in the back seat would be reduced to wrangling between themselves.

But Chris, never taking his eyes off the rear-view mirror, said with studied calm, "What is that supposed to mean, Bethany?"

Jessica's back stiffened. Perhaps Bethy saw that. In any case, they became less belligerent.

"I only meant — well, sometimes controversy helps. You had Mom say to the reporters at the hospital that you and she were always on the side of the field laborers, no matter what they did."

"And so we are," Chris admitted equably. "I came into office on that pledge, and I've always had their best interests at heart."

"Yes, but how can you keep saying that and still be so dead set against their joining a union? Everyone in the world belongs to a union of some kind. It's so medieval to hold out just because these people are migratory. Nobody's against collective bargaining these days. Even the most extreme conservatives know better."

Chris's expression scarcely changed as he said, apropos of nothing, "Robin, is that dirt on your upper lip? Or are you trying to grow a mustache?"

Bethy tittered as Robin replied stiffly, "I shaved off the mustache."

Jessica, sympathetic, came to his defense. "Actually, darling, the problem is that Robin hasn't shaved today."

At that, Chris smiled, said, "Sorry, boy," and peace reigned until they reached home in the Eastbay Hills.

Thank God, Jessica thought, at least Chris's mother would not be in from Tokyo until tomorrow. There would be enough to do, just getting the household reorganized after the long months during which the family had been separated by the children's schools and Chris's work in Washington.

The family was all shaken up as they entered the house by the message that Governor McClatchey had called twice and would talk to either Chris or Senator March.

"Beginning to feel his oats," Chris remarked shortly as he and Jessica read the messages.

Robin read over their shoulders. "I thought Old Sim was your boy."

"Kindly remember that *Old Sim* is younger than I am," Chris said automatically, but there was much truth in Robin's comment and Jessica looked at her husband with some anxiety.

"It couldn't be the interviews, could it?" she asked. "Everything was so careful. I can't see how there could have been a slipup."

"Oh, Mom!" Bethy cried. "Don't be so god-damned humble! You've gone overboard saying the right thing. Nobody can blame you." She glared at her father. "Nobody!"

To Jessica's relief, Chris chucked Bethy under her small pointed chin. "Now, don't get your dander up, Princess. I'm with you. Our Jess can do no wrong." He kissed Jessica on the forehead and then, to her surprise and the children's delight, on the lips. "I'll take the call in the den. You wait for me. There may be something you can tell Sim."

She went in obediently and sat on the arm of Chris's lounge chair while he put through the call to the ancient Governor's Mansion in Sacramento.

He still seems to be Chris's man, Jessica thought as the governor came on the line almost at once. But there was a little problem as usual. Jessica groaned when it turned out to be the old, old "little" problem. Complaints had reached the governor's desk from some of his biggest financial backers of the wine industry. It seemed Bick Haldean, their public enemy number two right after Juan Alvaro, was getting too many exclusives from Senator Jessica March. There was even a hint that Jessica and Bick had been "friends" over a long period of time.

"Of course, I'll deny it," Chris said firmly,

reasonably. "You ought to know that, Sim. What the devil does Haldean say about Senator March? No, no. I mean politically. Good God! Why would there be 'something between them?' She's my wife, isn't she?" He looked over the phone at Jessica. "Did you hear that, darling? Now, these mudslingers are trying to get up some dirt between you and that pinko writer. Nothing could be more ridiculous, Sim. She says she despises the fellow. Don't you, Jess?"

Jessica said nothing at all. She was speechless. But as Chris had gone right ahead with her supposed answer, she bit her tongue and remained silent. It seemed to her, in retrospect, however, that her own husband was implying that no man would possibly be having an affair with his wife, and that Jessica wouldn't attract the virile Haldean in any case.

"What else is bothering you, Sim?"

They talked a few minutes about Sim McClatchey's troubles with the new California budget which was now the biggest in the nation and causing bodies everywhere to turn over in their graves. But Jessica had lost interest when her own charms as a woman had been so easily swept under the table.

The conversation over, Chris took Jessica up to her pleasant, sunny bedroom suite with its early-American furniture and four-poster bed, its pewter collection which was her pride, and the friendly, homey look of the chintz covers. With a tired, happy sigh, Jessica looked around at the familiar objects and beyond to her dressing room and bathroom. She took off the jacket of her last-year's Chanel suit, fluffed up her hair and said, "I'd rather be here than in the White House."

Chris, who had pulled back the drapes to get the afternoon sun from a southerly direction and the city beyond, looked startled though he laughed.

"Careful, darling. Don't let President Walters hear you say that. Some day it may be a quote to haunt you."

Curious, Jessica thought, trying not to reveal her own ideas on the subject, after eighteen years, he doesn't really know me at all.

Bethy knocked but, finding her mother's door ajar, rushed in breathlessly.

"She's here! Wouldn't you know it? She couldn't show up when Mom was dying, but here she is now. And that disgusting Robin is positively fawning on her, asking all about Sikkim and Hindoostan and idiotic places like that!"

Jessica rushed to grab up her jacket while Chris gave his daughter a fatherly lecture on proper respect for her grandmother, and by the time Augusta March and Robin passed the open hall door the rest of the family was ready to show her the respect she required.

Chris March's mother was a fine-boned, elongated, and equally handsome female version of her distinguished son. Jessica knew this because she had read it, endlessly repeated, whenever the august Augusta appeared politically. She allowed her son to kiss her skillfully me-up cheek, pointed somewhere near that spot for Bethy to touch with her lips, and then graciously embraced Jessica.

Her pale blue eyes active over her daughter-in-law, Mrs. March said archly, "Nervous exhaustion! My dear, no one will believe it. You look as young, as Bethany. You must hate me for arriving a day too soon."

Everyone hurried to talk at once, assuring her she was mistaken, that they adored seeing her any time. Jessica wondered if they were all lying as she herself lied because the woman terrified her in some obscure way.

"But, really, I've no head for figures," Augusta March explained, waving graceful hands which were appropriately sheathed to the elbow in Dior gloves of pink kid. "I forgot about the International Dateline, so I'm either one day early or one day late, I forget which."

Jessica excused herself and went back to her room to change, while Robin and Chris, and even Bethy, a trifle shamefaced, trotted after Augusta to receive their souvenirs from the Far East.

Jessica began to unpack, although remembering the instructions that she must lie down when she reached home. Doctors were always so impractical; they hadn't the least notion of the fullness of a woman's day, especially when she had to be mother, wife, and senator. There was not too much to unpack, mostly bed jackets, satin and frilled, the chief gifts she had received, and the nightgowns, sheer and long the way she loved them. Here was the apricot one she wore the morning after her heart attack, the one that she was woman enough to know had its effect upon Bick Haldean, in spite of her husband's laughing disbelief in such a possibility.

The day of the attack itself was vague, even now. From the time she and Sue Lyburg got in the elevator and started down, it was almost a blank, a nightmarish series of shots like a movie montage, many faces peering at her out of the semidark of a cave. A cocktail bar? And then a moment of relief, the sight of Bethy's dear young face. And Bick, of course.

And the pain.

She saw her reflection in the long dressing-room mirror and remembering that pain, thinking, nervous exhaustion? In a pig's eye! But, of course, she must live

77

with that story from now on.

And some day, maybe, if I'm awfully lucky, we'll land in the White House!

Meanwhile, however, she was absolutely determined to outdo her mother-in-law. In spite of all the good manners between them, she always suspected Augusta March had, at the time of their marriage, despised the seventeen-year-old bride. In fact, to this day Jess was not sure why the woman had accepted her into the elegant, if poverty-stricken family. For this, among many reasons, it was absolutely necessary that Jessica keep her health — if only to spite her mother-in-law.

Dexter Dominik called at the house in person while Mrs. March was sorting out reminiscences and souvenirs, so Jessica inherited him. While they lived at home, the Marches, always aware of their image as a typical middle-class couple, had a cleaning woman and her assistant who came in twice a week, a cook who did not live in, and a yard man. Chris March's male secretary, Perce Maslington, often acted as his bartender, butler, doorman, and valet. As he was studying hard to follow in the boss's steps, Perce seemed perfectly willing to undergo all the intermediate discomforts.

Jessica came out at the top of the curving white staircase and as she started down, she saw with deep resentment that D.D. had brought a photographer with a small but highly useful camera with revolving flashcubes. He snapped shots of her as rapidly as possible, while D.D. kept saying, "Beautiful! Gorgeous! No one can say this is a sick woman!"

Jessica figured there was no use in telling him the staircase itself was forbidden to her and that a nurse would be here tomorrow, "just in case." Except for the various normal pressures of life, like her mother-in-law and Dexter Dominik, she did feel fine. In any event, the nurse would be referred to as "Senator March's Social Secretary," a kind of super Sue Lyburg.

"Is someone saying I'm a sick woman?" she asked lightly, taking D.D.'s outstretched hand but smiling in the direction of the photographer.

It occurred to her then that she had seen the little, effeminate-looking photographer at several Washington gatherings, that he not only peddled impromptu and often awkward shots of celebrities but also any nuggets of filth he could mine.

"Has Sim talked with you and Chris yet?" D.D. asked her under cover of the handshake. She nodded, and he added, "I suppose it was about the riot this morning. Keep in mind, the members are misguided. It's the leader who's planning the destruction of his own people. Typical commie tactics."

Bewildered, she tried to keep a knowledgeable look on her face, partly for the benefit of the nosy photographer but most of all because she didn't want D.D. to think he was springing anything on her unexpectedly. From the hints he gave her, it seemed likely that the riot concerned Alvaro and the farm laborers. Much as she sympathized with the migrant workers with whom her father had once had much in common, she felt that other problems deserved at least some attention.

"Surely," she said, raising her voice, "there must be something else going on in the world besides Alvaro and the farm laborers. Can't we worry about the bomb, or Red China, or the militant blacks, or when the moon will be colonized?"

"Jess . . ." D.D. began.

She recognized the tone of warning and resented it wildly but was careful not to lose her temper in public.

The photographer's pale, pimpled face beamed until his little eyes were enclosed in bundles of flesh. He seemed to be eager to agree with her, which was nice but did put her on her guard. "That sounds like a very sensible remark, senator. After all, there really are more important things in the world than the migrant worker problem."

"I learned, during my few weeks in the Senate this spring, that there are forty-nine other states," she said, ignoring D.D., "and they all have problems, some of which transcend their state borders. Why must we always return to that fellow? He's not God, you know."

D.D. put in smoothly, "Senator March means to say that the condition of the laborers themselves is more important to her than the ambitions of rabble-rousing pinkos like Juan Alvaro who have stirred up the entire state."

The little bug eyes of the photographer shifted to Jessica. "That is what you meant to say, senator?"

For a count of roughly five, Jessica was caught with her mouth open, caught for posterity by a camera and flash, while she tried to agree with D.D. and still remain true to her own deep and, she hoped very personal, beliefs. She moistened her lips nervously.

"I mean simply that all I have ever heard about Mr. Alvaro was things like this: riots, people hurt, things like that." She hurried on: "If only Mr. Alvaro could meet with the wine-growers!" She laughed, saw the two men look at her curiously. "I mean — we women believe in compromise. We think that it is better than

81

riots and killings and that sort of thing."

The little man squinted at D.D., then, letting his thick pink lips ripple above his teeth, he smiled. "Compromise. That is your stand. Very feminine. Does Senator — ah — Secretary of the Interior March subscribe to your belief in compromise?"

Angered by this prodding from two sides, she snapped, "You asked me what my stand was. I've told you. The Secretary of the Interior will give you his own answers."

D.D. said placatingly, "That is because the senator and the secretary think alike in so many ways. You've seen that from the beginning of the secretary's career."

The little man said, "Oh? Is this a fact, senator? You've no objection to a quote to that effect, I suppose."

By this time she had gotten control of herself and managed to calm down. But if only, she thought, trying not to look nervous, if only I could speak for myself just once!

She surprised herself by the cool confidence her voice demonstrated after that unfortunate burst of frankness. "If you quote me as saying my husband and I agree that my first concern is the welfare of the people of California, then that seems a fair summation."

"Such a nice vocabulary, senator! You went

to Cal like your son, didn't you?"

D.D. put in hastily, breathing fast, "Before Berkeley went communist. Mrs. March went to Cal only one year, isn't that so?"

Jessica had never despised herself so much as in this moment when she tacitly agreed, hearing Chris's and Augusta's footsteps on the stairs behind her. "Yes. I — I didn't go there very long, a little less than a year."

"Before it went communist," D.D. nailed in his "facts."

"Before —" She bit that off. "None of my schoolmates were communists. You can quote that." What difference did it make? They could be green-eyed dragons. They had been her friends . . . like Bick Haldean.

Into the tight little group stepped Chris and his handsome mother. He looked just a trifle upset, probably because the photographer had brought up the subject of the university. This was always a sore spot because he too had gone to Berkeley, and his bachelor's degree was from Cal. But Augusta, now deceptively soft in a hostess gown of pink nylon and lace, her gray-blonde hair regally wound in its habitual French twist, murmured, "What are we thinking of? Why are we all so serious? Shouldn't we all have a little something to drink? Some sherry? A gin and tonic, or whatever?"

Jessica shook herself hastily. "Yes. I'll go and see about it." Anything to get out of this squeeze play between her husband and mother-in-law on one side, the thick-lipped photographer and D.D. on the other. But when she went into the charming little paneled bar, hardly bigger than a closet, behind the staircase, she found Robin and Bethany there before her, efficiently organizing a tray with decanters and mixes and fussing over a bucket of ice cubes.

"You're getting the ice all salty," Robin complained. "Cry into the sherry. It's too strong anyway. Gram always puts ice in hers."

Sure enough, when Jessica in great concern turned her daughter gently to face her, Bethy's big eyes were red-rimmed and she was sniffling angrily. Before Jessica could ask what was wrong, Robin slammed down some ice tongs for emphasis.

"The joker's safe! He's not dead. So what's to bawl?"

"Who?" For a ghastly few seconds Jessica thought they were talking about Bick Haldean and was shaken by her own violent reactions.

Bethy shrugged with helpless rage at her own tears and got out her complaint in a shattered voice: "All he was doing — all — was just passing out pamphlets at the gate of the Croisetti Farms. Just that! And some bullyboys in boots and crash helmets started hitting everyone on the head. He just missed getting his head bashed in . . . and then they arrest *him* for disturbing the peace!"

Robin put in, "But he'll be out before tonight. Wait and see. That's the thing. Bick Haldean called a few minutes ago and told us about it. Funny, though. Sometimes you get a feeling even Alvaro's life is in danger."

Jessica, who had been shaking, leaned back against the bar and fanned herself with a cocktail napkin.

"For God's sake! Are you talking about that Alvaro man?"

Cut to the quick, Bethy cried, "Well, of course! Who else? I should have been there. I'd intended to be."

"Very likely." Jessica had gotten hold of herself and took the tray from Robin, but then she hesitated, kissed Bethy briskly and added in a softer voice, "I'm glad you weren't there, Princess. I need you here."

Bethy blew her nose on a handkerchief provided by her brother with friendly disgust, and the children followed Jessica out to entertain the photographer and Dexter Dominik who went overboard trying out his charm on Bethy, but all in vain.

The photographer proved to be only the first visitor of the day, and Jessica was relieved that, so far as he could tell, she made no more bloopers that day — not as much might be said for Bethy who couldn't be silenced even by her father.

It seemed extraordinary to Jessica as the evening wore on that she had not thought all day of the coming night with her husband. She had thought so often of it in the hospital. There were so many months lately during which she slept alone that she had been almost happy over the heart attack because it brought Chris home, but tonight, belatedly, as she confessed to Augusta, "I feel like a bride again."

"And you're actually blushing! My dear girl, at your age!" Augusta remarked laughing a little.

This made Jessica glance quickly at the mirror of her dressing table where she sat brushing her hair with long, languid strokes. The view that came back to her was a big improvement over the woman Bick Haldean saw the day of her heart attack. The eyes returning her gaze seemed to catch the sparkle from the makeup lamps. They looked excited, and like the full curves of her mouth, sensuous. She was careful to wear the sheer apricot nightgown which was of a color and empire style that had always roused Chris's libido at this hour of the night.

Augusta stood up, impressing Jessica as always by her height and her dignity that was impervious to outside influence. She rested her hand on Jessica's nearly bare shoulder. This, Jessica thought, was the crux of Augusta March's "woman-to-woman" visit tonight which, until this moment, had pointless chatter. Mrs. March seldom did anything pointlessly.

"Jessica, you've been a good wife to my son. Better than I —" she paused just a fraction of time, "others might have been. I hope you will continue to be so."

"I have done the best I could to carry on for Chris," Jessica reminded her stiffly.

Augusta raised her fingers slowly, one at a time. "No, dear. I wasn't thinking of that. I mean, you must be broadminded about his ambition. Anything else would be disastrous. Well . . . a word to the wise . . . good night." She kissed the air lightly near Jessica's right cheek and left for the room reserved for her upon her frequent visits to the Bay area. Her home was in Maryland just outside Washington. In many ways she saw Chris nowadays more than his senator-wife did. She had been a national committeewoman and now was on a presidential fact-finding commission and having a ball as she circled the globe, offering advice and making full reports to President

Walters on overseas-aid programs. Her advice was generally more succinct than her expression of it. She was against the programs.

She heard her husband's footsteps now on the old-fashioned polished hardwood floor of his bedroom and was aware of a glow that suffused her body as she waited for him to open the dressing room door between them which she had left ajar. Because she was exceedingly conscious of their long separation now, it seemed a very long time before he appeared in the doorway smiling at her, looking trim, beautifully muscled, wearing tailored pajama pants with the jacket thrown over his arm as in the old days. He gestured with the arm, shaking the tailored blue silk jacket.

"Remember when I had to have the jacket handy? They were always calling me out of bed at two A.M. to save them from being carted back to Mexico."

"I was never more proud of you all the same." She looked up at him as he leaned over the bed. She told herself everything was as it had been during those passionate, romantic nights, and often days, early in their marriage.

"He'll go far, that fellow," her mother had assured her in that practical way Thea Gribble Souza always looked at life.

Jessica raised her head, her mouth quivering a little, betraying the inner cravings, the long starvation that — surely? — Chris shared. She did not make the aggressive move as she might have done with inducement from a man of Bick Haldean's type. She knew Chris well enough to understand that in their open signs of affection, including kisses, he preferred to initiate the actions as he initiated all their love-play. Once it had mattered greatly. She was a passionate woman as she had been a passionate girl, and this problem of playing the "passive wife" had been the first real problem of her marriage.

Chris's face approached hers, and she felt his lips brush her own, then, having aroused her to that pitch of longing and desire which had once been in his power, he moved away, went around to the opposite side of the bed and reached up to snap off the pink-glowing lamp. But his hand stopped in mid motion as he saw the evening's copy of the influential *Oakland Tribune* which he had already studied before dinner. It was perfectly understandable that Chris should be interested. On the front page was a handsome shot of Chris assisting a healthily smiling Jessica out of the wheel chair which the hospital insisted she use to reach the March Oldsmobile. Vaguely in the background were Bethy and Robin looking anxious.

Chris looked at the paper for a minute or

two, refolded it, and set it back in place under the lamp. Then he snapped off the lamp. That long few minutes had a chilling effect on Jessica's mood. It reminded her forceably of many failures in their love-making, especially during their Washington years together.

When the lamp went off, the room was at once edged in moonlight. The distant black silhouette of the city of Oakland, divisive, concerned with endless problems of race and economics, seemed to haunt Jessica. She wished suddenly that the early-American chintz drapes had been thicker. She didn't want the world to intrude upon these moments, the first really private time she had enjoyed with her husband in months.

Chris reached over to draw her to him. His love-making had always been brisk, short, very much to the point of pleasing himself, but there was always in Jessica, a deep feeling of gratitude that this handsome, popular man had chosen the Portuguese laborer's daughter to be his wife. Besides, he was very likely one of those men whose sexual drive was just not great; it had been channeled into his far-greater political drive . . . unless, he was finding satisfaction elsewhere.

Tonight she welcomed his body with all her own passion that had for so long been stifled. It was a mistake, as her instinct told her almost at once. Chris still preferred the passive woman. His climax was reached and he was sated while her own emotions remained unsatisfied.

Afterward he remained beside her for perhaps ten minutes, then gave her a perfunctory good-night kiss, said, "Good to have my girl well again," and left her.

She lay there a long time in the moonlight, wondering why moments she waited for with such anticipation, could prove so unfulfilling.

Would it have been like this if I had married Bick?

Then she closed her eyes and her mind to this adulterous thought and fell asleep.

- SIX -

For the next few days Chris did what Jessica considered an enormous favor: he borrowed her secretary, Sue Lyburg, and they took care of a great deal of Jessica's official mail and paperwork. Sue had worked for Chris in Washington briefly the past spring and seemed to take his dictation readily, not even objecting to the irregular hours and the night work.

Jessica, meanwhile, busied herself with getting the household back in running order, persuading Robin to live home during his vacation instead of remaining in Berkeley, and welcoming Bethany back from her fashionable girls' school in Marin County. Though it was wonderful to have the children with her, Jess hadn't realized the turmoil their presence would cause when they were both so wrapped up in causes and demonstrations. Even that got to be commonplace, but there was always an unpleasant undercurrent between them and their father. Chris tried not to arouse the children by any violent antagonism, but Jess often suspected it was as much his good manners and lack of interest as his fatherly concern that kept him even from arguing with them.

Augusta March claimed the children lacked respect; yet, somehow, they often seemed to like their grandmother better than their own father, a fact which Jessica resented for Chris. Augusta had postponed her departure from day to day while she made public appearances on Jessica's behalf, but finally a summons from her committee in Washington proved insurmountable, and she prepared to leave. Jessica drove her to the airport when a call from Herb Millvale, the presidential assistant, delayed Chris.

"Be sure and let me know what The Man has to say to you, dear," was his final goodbye from his mother. "Call me tomorrow at the country place." This was her Maryland estate.

Chris, busy putting a report together for briefing of the White House, kissed his wife and Augusta and sent them on their way while he arranged for Sue Lyburg to record his full telephone conversation.

"Do you really mind it very much?" Augusta asked abruptly while they waited for the calling of Mrs. March's plane.

Startled, Jessica wondered if the woman was a mind reader — or did she simply know her son was not a complete success in the romantic department? After all, Jess thought resentfully, he's no longer a boy. He can't be perfect.

"I've always considered myself lucky to be Chris's wife. As far as I'm concerned, he suits me perfectly."

Mrs. March massaged her gloved fingers, first one hand, then the other, until the exquisite kid covering was almost entirely free of wrinkles. Jess was sure this was to avoid her daughter-in-law's eyes.

"I meant, of course, do you mind this political rat race you've been thrust into? I tried to tell Christopher it was a mistake, that you simply were not cut out for this business, but —" She shrugged eloquently. "You really have to be born to it . . . and I don't mean that the way it sounds, my dear."

Determined not to be put down as she had been long ago in their early relationship, Jess asked cuttingly, "Don't you? How *do* you mean it to sound, dear?"

"Quite simply, you're too nice for it. Now," she presented her cheek for the airy kiss, "they're calling my plane. You mustn't be angry with me, Jess. Believe me, I have your interests very much at heart. Why," she waved her hands, "without you, I can honestly say, there would probably have been no political career for Christopher — not, at least, so soon. And that, my dear, was one of my son's great assets at the beginning: his youth."

She rattled on in the same vein as Jess walked to the gate with her, not listening too closely. She was thinking that Chris had made a serious miscalculation in choosing her, rather than his mother when he needed a political tool. But there was also triumph in that choice. At least it meant that he preferred his wife and trusted his wife before his mother.

Another, and rather nasty alternative occurred to her now: had it been simply that his mother was already in a position that could influence people toward his candidacy, so he used his wife as his second tool?

"Well," Augusta said finally, with brisk pleasantness, "Good-bye again, dear. Take care of yourself and the children. Don't let Chris work you too hard. And remember what I said. We owe you a great deal, so you may imagine how proud we are going to be over your part in Christopher's triumph this November."

What the devil does she mean: they owe me a great deal? Because I took over like a robot as Senator March? But she herself wanted that job! Whet else, then?

She gave up. Augusta March was fond of being cryptic. It added to her mystique. Jess waved a kiss to the handsome woman striding across the field because she not only feared and envied Mrs. March, she also admired her.

A rough hand reached over her shoulder and closed on her wrist, waving her hand mechanically as an adult waves a child's hand.

"What —" She looked around into Bick Haldean's face which was so close his chin scraped her cheek. His mouth looked as rough as his face, but his eyes were warm; they might be said to have smiled at her. Quite suddenly, and apropos of nothing, she felt again in her memory the pressure of that mouth of his upon hers the night in the Oakland Hills when she was seventeen and she relived the feel of those hard, rough, vital hands upon her body that made her at once his property and his protected love. What a fool she had been! So frightened! So panicked! Not guessing that nearly twenty years later she would trade a good deal of her tepid, sterile life for the sensuous delights she had missed. But then there was a great deal more to marriage than sex. Bick would probably have made a very bad husband . . . wouldn't he?

And then another thrill, this time of something very like terror: the thought of Bick eying young Bethany, ready to take up where he left off with Bethy's mother?

Bick had started to speak to Jess but something in her expression made him blink and wait for a moment until she smiled.

"Hello, Bick. I didn't expect to see you here cheering on my mother-in-law."

"Cheering her out of California? Nothing would suit me better. I'd nominate her for the White House if I thought it would keep her away from here."

"Shhh!" Jessica looked around with an air of conspiracy. "People will think you got your political education from the candidate's wife."

"You're more right than you think, Jess . . . Look across the field."

Uneasy, she looked. There was her mother-in-law on the top step, about to disappear into the big jet. But she had stopped, shaded her eyes with her gloved hand, and was staring hard at Jessica and Bick.

"Mind?" Bick asked lightly.

"Not at all." She wasn't sure what was coming but was in a strange mood and added with a devilish gleam, "Show me what I should mind."

He cupped her chin in the palm of his big hand and kissed her a little too heartily to suggest whatever smoldering passion might be hidden beneath their mischievous, public gesture. Over her head, he looked at the distant witness.

Jess said, "What's she doing?"

He grinned. "She's just made a fist — either that, or she's badly shaken. That does it. She's gone. We scared her away. What a shame! I could have gone on like this for hours." He kissed her again, attracting several passersby who glanced at them, with amused sympathy, supposing them to be lovers about to part.

"I'm being hopelessly compromised," she reminded him, having been kissed too quickly to get a chance to respond.

"I hope so. But you see, it was all worth it to get that gorgeous look in your eyes again." He turned her toward the mirrored showcase nearby and she had to admit the face she had grown accustomed to was improved, particularly in spirit. Jessica March was often referred to in print as "beautiful Senator March" but, as was frequently pointed out, she was not only one of the youngest senators extant, but had little competition in the beauty department. Whatever common sense and modesty might do to counteract what she saw, Jessica thought with considerable pleasure that she had never looked better.

"Come along," Bick told her with rough humor. "Stop admiring yourself and let me introduce you to somebody."

Her thought, momentarily, was of this being some political move, the way Chris so often made use of her. Then, squaring her shoulders and looking her attractive best, she took Bick's arm.

"Friend of yours?"

"Yes, and I want you to be nice to her."

She was feeling such a lift of the spirit that she bragged laughingly, "Why not? I'm a very nice girl."

"I've always known that, Jess — since you were sixteen. Too bad you didn't know I could be nice."

"Seventeen. And don't tell me you haven't enjoyed all the delights of bachelorhood in the meantime." Nevertheless, she sneaked a side look at him, hoping womanlike to hear a denial.

His smile was more grim than she had expected.

"It is possible to get tired of waiting. I've *waited* over a good deal of this cracked and shriveled planet. It's a good thing you age attractively."

That word *age* made her cringe inwardly as she saw herself in his eyes, aging, growing sick, thin, with bad color and lackluster complexion, and soon, graying hair. But the way he had expressed himself left a clear suggestion that he still cared for her. She knew she was being a dog in the manger. She had a husband who might have married any girl and miraculously had married her. It was understandable that Chris no longer felt a white-hot teenage passion for her. In some ways, he never had;

he wasn't a passionate man. But it warmed her entire body, and sometimes her spirits, to realize that Bick still felt for her a little of his own youthful passion. She knew now that her own passions were not as well under control as she had supposed they were.

She began to wonder who this friend of Bick's might be, and why she was particularly asked to be pleasant. She hoped she was always pleasant to strangers. Friends, it is true, might see another side of her temper. But strangers!

"Who's your friend, Bick?"

"Not exactly a friend, I can't flatter myself she knows me well enough."

The idea hit her at the same time that she saw the woman they were to meet, a strikingly beautiful dark woman at the baggage counter who waved and called to Bick. Italian, probably. Or Portuguese? No, a softer edge, a woman whose ancestors belonged here long before Bick and even Jess Souza's father. The woman was of Mexican descent although obviously from her voice she was born in the United States. It wasn't this idea which hit Jess with such force but the realization that after all these years, Bick Haldean must have found a replacement for the seventeen-year-old Jess Souza. She made up her mind to be so nice he would never guess the shock to her.

Yes, she lashed herself, you really are

a dog in the manger, Jess.

"Come along, Jess. She won't bite. I guar-
antee it. Her manners are quite as good as
yours. Maybe better."

He misunderstood entirely. Jess hurried her
steps. "No, really, she's lovely. You're very
lucky, Bick. Why have you kept it a secret?
I would love to meet —"

"Elena! Good to see you. Never mind the
baggage. Give me your claim check. This is
Jessica March."

Elena smiled with a surprising effort, Jess
thought as she held out her own hand.

"Yes, I recognize you, senator." She
stepped back from the counter making room
for Bick which left the women in an awkward
twosome a little to one side of the crowd.

Jess, feeling the awkwardness and made uneasy by it, suspected that the other woman
resented the seeming intimacy between Jess
and Bick. She tried to clear this up at once.

"I've known Bick since I was in school.
Seems a long time now."

"Surely not, senator," said the woman politely.

"Have you — have you known him — for
a long time I mean." What the devil makes
me so gauche, so clumsy? Jess asked herself.

The woman glanced back over her shoulder
at Bick and then, as if she suddenly understood, broke into a genuine smile.

"Bick is a devil, you know. He did this deliberately, failed to introduce us. Wanted to watch the explosion, I suppose. He is writing a series of articles on my husband's life. My husband is Juan Alvaro."

Jessica gasped and tried to cover that quick, involuntary reaction. "How do you do? You must be very proud of your husband. He is a great hero to my young daughter . . . that is," as the woman's dark eyes gazed at her, hooded by their heavy eyelids, "I should say, he is much admired. And anyone who can measure up to the children's beliefs and hopes today must be a remarkable man."

"I think so," said Mrs. Alvaro. "And I think you are a fair woman, senator. At least Bick tells me so."

What was Bick up to? He had maneuvered this meeting somehow and for some purpose. Him and his damned causes! Men Bick's age forgot causes and got down to cases. But as she tried hard to put her best foot forward with Elena Alvaro, she knew she was actually glad that Bick Haldean had never grown up.

"Ah," said Bick innocently coming between the two wives with Mrs. Alvaro's suitcase and tote bag. "I see you two girls are old buddies by now. Took me a little longer to get the bags than I'd expected. Terrific crowd."

"You conniving rat!" Jess told him pleasantly, a remark that was echoed by Mrs. Alvaro in rapid Spanish.

It was perfectly evident that the two women had been connived into treating each other with civility. In the end the whole thing went much further than Jess had intended it to go.

For some curious reason, as Jess discovered when they were on their way to the parking lot, Bick Haldean had come all the way across the Bay and out to the airport in a cab, and would have to take Mrs. Alvaro back to her home fifty miles north of San Francisco in the same unorthodox way. Jess made up her mind not to be further manipulated or stampeded into Bick's plans. She got clear to her car in the lot, accompanied "to be sure nothing happens to you" by Bick and an amused, if reluctant, Mrs. Alvaro, when she caught Elena Alvaro's eyes, and both women laughed. Bick's scheme, whatever it was, had worked.

"Do let me drive you wherever you're going, both of you," Jess offered as graciously as possible under the circumstances.

While Bick made the most flimsy excuses before putting the other woman in the front seat, Mrs. Alvaro, with a significant look at Jess, said, "We may as well let you. I have a suspicion that before Bick is done with us we are meant to be the best of friends."

"I'd like that very much," Jess agreed with

103

more politeness than feeling. She had a nerve-racking notion that somewhere along the line she was being used to betray her own and her husband's ideals, or if not their ideals, at least their principles. The thing that puzzled her, but only momentarily, was whether all her own ideals and principles coincided with Chris's.

Although the ride was a pleasant one and the company surprisingly good, Jess found herself wondering now and then if Bick Haldean's entire interest in the Alvaro cause had its inception in the beauty of Elena Alvaro. She could hardly blame him. His basic beliefs and interests, whatever their motives, were deeply felt, she was sure. He had always been like that, even when she first knew him. It had prejudiced her mother against him in some ways, though Thea Gribble Souza was always fair, whatever her conflicts between emotion and common sense.

In the car Elena Alvaro and Jess talked of the young people involved in various causes that season, causes having proved, to Jess's cynical view, seasonal in their popularity. Mrs. Alvaro was quiet, pleasant, and sincere in discussing Bethany March's work for her husband's collective-bargaining cause, but it humiliated Jess to be told so much about her own daughter, and it also opened up what Bick agreed, from the back seat, was going to be a whole new can of peas.

"Mrs. Alvaro, I think the most important thing my daughter can do is to complete her precollegiate education. If she keeps cutting school, she is not going to be prepared to enter college next year."

They were driving up through the lovely, still-green country north of Marin County, a countryside famed almost since California's statehood for its superb table wines, and it was hard to believe that such loveliness bred conditions similar to those of the migrant workers in the arid vastness of the San Joaquin Valley.

It soon became evident that Elena Alvaro was also occupied with thoughts of this anomaly.

"I agree that Miss March's education is important — even supremely important. But I assure you, that lovely girl is now aware of a much greater world than the small, correct, bookish world she reads about in that young ladies' school."

"You make it sound like a nineteenth-century seminary," Jessica objected, resenting the implied criticism of Chris's educational plans. "It's a very good school with a high rating nationally." The awkward thing about her defense of Bethy's school was that Jess herself had been violently opposed to a snobbish school full of rich people's children, and no boys either, where she was liable to get a complex.

Whatever had happened in that girls' school, it certainly hadn't given Bethy a complex about boys, unless it made her prefer men . . . like Bick. On second thought, her preference for older men might be the result of a complex.

Mrs. Alvaro made no more criticisms of Bethy's schooling but began to point out an impressive series of low, rolling hillsides, beautifully cultivated, with the young grapes well along to maturity and not growing, as Jess had always supposed, on long, trailing vines. In the far distance, half hidden by a fold in the hillside, was the second story of a large white frame house which the rising highway revealed a minute later as built in an antebellum style with porticos and pillars and everything but the stars-and-bars.

"The Croisetti Farms headquarters," Mrs. Alvaro explained. "But the original Italian family no longer controls the company . . . a New York syndicate makes the policies now."

Jessica looked across the perfect acreage where a few workers between geometric rows seemed to be casually examining the vines.

She couldn't help remarking, "There doesn't seem to be much misery, overwork, or extreme poverty there. My husband is responsible for much of what you see there, the good conditions for employees, the clean work . . ."

Bick started to say something but bit it off and pretended to cough, and Elena Alvaro understood clearly that she was selected to answer.

"I know. Fifteen years ago we all thought your husband was to be the savior of the Mexican-American and all the migrant workers. That civil rights and the rest of it could be circumvented. We believed that giving those people the right to vote — many of them hardly able to read or write — would put them in the hands of demagogues. We thought, even I thought, they were not yet educated enough to know what was good for them, collective bargaining, all the rest. So we voted for Congressman March, then Senator March, then people like Governor McClatchey because Senator March told us to do so."

"Well?" Jessica asked, trying to be reasonable and yet to remind her of what the Southwest and California owed to the Marches. "Almost all of Chris's public life has been spent talking about what was good for his Mexican-American constituents."

"*His* constituents," echoed Mrs. Alvaro quietly. "And now, times have changed. These American citizens do know how to vote, how to decide what is best for them. Your husband sounds exactly like those labor leaders we were afraid of in the beginning. But his friends, the Duvauxs, the Clormanns who are the new owners of Croisetti Farms, some of the others, they hold your husband's constituents in peonage. *Peonage!* There is simply no other word for it. And all their work is being done from outside the state, outside the United States, by poor, unfortunate people who are unprotected, who are left to starve, and who, at the same time, are keeping our citizens, your husband's constituents, from working." She broke off abruptly. "I'm sorry. I am not usually the speechmaker of the family." She lowered her head and stared through the windshield, then out the open window beyond the boundaries of the neat, clean Croisetti lands as if searching for something. She must have found it because she said with a new urgency, "They say one picture is worth a thousand words. Would you mind turning at the next road to your right? The dirt road beyond those hedgerows."

Groaning privately, Jess turned in silence and without the polite disclaimer that "it was no trouble." It was a farm road, dusty, rutted, with the thrills of a roller coaster across the uneven terrain. The Croisetti Farm bordered the road on the south, and Mrs. Alvaro explained that the Verona Wineries were to the north. "Not so neat," she said, "but they do pay better." As though, Jess thought, there were some connection between neatness and low pay!

"What are we looking for?" she asked finally, her temper ragged after this latest bouncing ride.

"I hope to find — you see, some of them usually wait along this road in the back country, hoping to be hired, or hiding from the immigration board. People bring them food, a few things."

"Do the employers know about t h e s e places?"

Bick laughed. "Do they know? They come to such places to get labor in season. Who do you think tells these poor devils about such places to hide?"

"There!" Elena cried. "Behind that huge oak tree on the north side."

An ancient Ford station wagon was parked under the tree whose great spreading branches almost concealed the wagon and its human contents from the sight of an unknowing passerby. Jess counted first seven, then ten, and finally eleven people, most of them young adult Mexicans with a strong strain of Indian blood, but there were three who were less than teenagers, mere children, dark-faced with huge hungry eyes that looked up at Jess and her companions in terror.

Someone was cooking pinto beans in a huge blackened kettle over a campfire. It didn't look like there were very many beans for eleven hungry bodies. Previously made and ready to wrap around the beans were eleven tortillas.

Jess winced and said, "Tell them we don't want to cause them any trouble. That isn't much to eat. Are all their meals for the day so meager?"

Bick and Mrs. Alvaro, having gotten out of the car, looked at each other. The woman said without expression, "This very probably is their only meal for the day." She looked over at the boy about ten who had started to hide behind the wagon but came out slowly, coaxed by Jess's painful smile and the warm, outthrusted hand of Elena Alvaro. Jess was too embarrassed at her own intrusion in their lives to look at the silent, staring, obviously nervous men at the campfire, but she could not resist the brave little boy. Mrs. Alvaro asked the boy something in Spanish.

The boy's beautiful brown eyes stared at

110

the intruders, each in turn, then, in a voice that made it sound commonplace, he said something very simply.

"Yes," Mrs. Alvaro said in her quiet way, turning to Jess. "He says this is today's food." The boy saw Bick grin at him, and the child grinned back enchantingly. He nodded his tousled head toward the kettle and added in fair English, "And good, no?"

"Smells great," Bick agreed and some of the broad-cheeked Indian faces around the kettle looked at him. The smiles seemed pitifully shy to Jess. Bick said to Mrs. Alvaro, "Hadn't we better let them know we aren't here to make trouble?"

Elena said something to the men who shifted uneasily, glancing at each other as if waiting for someone else to speak for them. A boy about Robin's age, stepped forward, pushing aside the little boy who had clearly fallen for the charms of Bick. Jess was surprised that he, and the others, were dressed the way Robin dressed when he was on one of his protest marches. But where Robin looked sloppy with his Aloha shirt tails flapping, his huaraches dusty, and his sensitive blond face merely unshaven, the appearance of these confused, nervous, desperately hopeful men was genuine. There was no effort to look picturesque, colorful, admired by fellow rebels.

These were the Real Ones. Jess wished suddenly that Robin could meet and know these people.

Bick explained, cutting into Jessica's painful thoughts, "They hoped we were going to hire them. If they aren't hired tomorrow, there is nothing left."

Anger washed away some of Jessica's embarrassment at her own guilt. "Who brought them here, or encouraged them to come? Why are they here if they haven't been hired?"

Elena explained, "They were smuggled up from a place near Mexicali to Livermore, across the Bay in a camper, on the promise of jobs. This ancient wagon is what they have lived in since then. The owner of the wagon seems to have vanished. He represented certain unnamed Californians."

"All eleven of them were smuggled in one camper?"

Elena ignored this as a foolish question. "The agent who took them over from the fellow who smuggled them in tells them now they won't be working until next month."

"Good God! Isn't there anything that can be done? Arrest the agent or the smuggler, or whatever?"

Mrs. Alvaro did not answer this. She went over to talk to the men at the bean pot, while

Bick reminded Jess softly, "Not as long as Senator March supports these smugglers and these agents. Who do you think most of these agents work for?"

"Chris never heard of them!"

"Honey, lie to yourself, but don't kid an old pro."

It is a frame-up, she told herself. Coming up here, detouring along this godforsaken byway. And these — there was no going on with that line of thought. One look at these painfully hopeful dark faces, the dream not quite killed that brought them to this desolation, and Jess knew she could not blame Mrs. Alvaro or even Bick. She wanted very much to go home and think . . . and then get some facts.

"Can we help them?" she asked as Bick and Mrs. Alvaro got back in the car. It was actually the fear and the desperate hope in the eyes of those men that haunted her even more than their physical hunger.

"There will be food tomorrow," the woman told her. "But these are only eleven souls. There are hundreds like that. They are brought in every year: innocent, ignorant, hopeful, used or not used, according to a whim or a sudden slowdown in the vineyards and the wineries and the fields. Don't you see how much we need organizing? Decent conditions that the owners must abide by? Not this smuggling of helpless, ignorant —"

"I know. I know!" Jess started up the car hurriedly, her hands shaking.

Surely Chris didn't know about this!

- SEVEN -

After a pregnant silence, as they drove out into the main highway, Mrs. Alvaro said hesitantly, "I hope you won't think this was an isolated case. You will find poor devils like these from here to Livermore or Stockton, poor deceived men dumped out of panel trucks or hauling trailers, half-dead of thirst, confused and hungry . . ."

Jess had not looked inside that old station wagon in which eleven people lived. She was almost glad she had not, although a thirst for knowledge was usually as strong in her as a physical thirst. Getting her thoughts together, Jess suspected there was some loophole somewhere. The wineries couldn't afford to pay the standard legal wages and keep in business. She had often been told that. But then, wasn't there something wrong in businesses that couldn't make a profit except under such conditions? It seemed to her, when she met Mrs. Gladys Duvaux, for instance, that the woman looked uncommonly prosperous. And so had some of the other wives.

Suddenly Jess sat up straighter. Bick noticed her stiff movement and asked with an anxiety that warmed her, "Are you all right, honey?"

Jess glanced at his reflection in the rear-view mirror. She had gotten over her irritation at Mrs. Alvaro. Once again with the thought of Gladys Duvaux came a prickling sensation of danger, something half-forgotten, a dream of voices in a dark cave that stank of wine and Bourbon and mink stoles . . .

"Yes, I'm fine. It's just that the Duvaux woman was in my dream."

"Dream?" Mrs. Alvaro looked at her curiously but Bick leaned forward over the back of Jessica's seat. He seemed more intent than a simple dream warranted.

"What about your dream? Was it the one you talked about the other day? A warning, you said?"

"Yes . . . no. I seem to have it all tangled up with the day I had my —" She stopped only just in time to keep from revealing the seriousness of her illness to the Alvaros, the worst enemy of the Marches. "I had a terrific case of nervous exhaustion, they called it — but it was mostly heartburn. Anyway I can't really think clearly about that day."

"Turn to your right as we enter town," said Mrs. Alvaro, "to that frame house just across the bridge."

It was a small, warm, tree-lined town, not too different from the way it might have looked in the era of Mexican California. They crossed a plaza with thick greenery in the center, and the park looked cool and welcoming. It was not crowded: a few dreaming old men, some children giggling loudly as they chased after a boy in a costume that was half astronaut, half frogman; there were no women. Probably home working, thought Jess cynically.

The Alvaro house, a large bungalow, was in a slight depression beyond the paved wooden bridge over a lackadaisical stream. A minute later when Jess drove between the low, open, white gates, she saw that the Alvaro house backed on the stream, and somewhere nearby there was the pleasant hum of summer insects among the grape and berry vines. Jess pulled up into the area in front of the little garage already crowded by three American cars. It was all much too bucolic and too perfect, except for those rich cars. No doubt she was intended to meet Juan Alvaro inside that happy home and change the ideas and policies of a lifetime. It was surprisingly transparent for a man of Bick's normal cleverness.

Elena Alvaro, however, got out before Bick could open the door, and then leaned across the front seat to ask Jess without really expecting an enthusiastic assent, "Will you come inside — meet my husband? For a moment or two? He will want to thank you."

"I thought your husband was — I'm sorry, Mrs. Alvaro, but my daughter seemed so concerned about your husband's arrest, so, naturally, I thought —"

Mrs. Alvaro looked at Bick. "He really was freed this morning? His telegram said so."

For the first time since she met him at the airport, Bick had the decency to look uneasy, unsure of his next move. He glanced over at the black Cadillac, the out-of-date but well-kept Chrysler Imperial, and a year-old Ford. Watching him as he assured Mrs. Alvaro that her husband had been publicly and heroically bailed out of jail, Jessica wondered why those cars — visitors obviously — bothered him. Even democratic demagogues like Juan Alvaro had a perfectly legitimate right to friends who drove Cadillacs. There was no law, as yet, against it.

Up until now, Jess had intended to defy all Bick's obvious schemes to have her meet Juan Alvaro, but seeing that Bick was so clearly upset by these cars, she decided to get out and meet the owners. It would be exciting to outwit Bick in this way. Elena Alvaro was moving hurriedly across the grass beyond the asphalt paving, and Jess made out the stern aristocratic face of Juan Alvaro behind the old-

118

fashioned screen door. His features softened as he caught sight of his wife, and he pushed open the screen door which made a screeching protest as he stepped out to embrace Elena.

They exchanged small, quick phrases in Spanish that reminded Jess of her father's endearing remarks to her mother who was not Portuguese but had long before learned to decode these romantic and very personal phrases. Her father, a short, stout, curly haired man of the soil, had not looked in the least like the lean and handsome *caballero* who was Juan Alvaro. Ironic, she thought, that a man of Alvaro's elegance should lay his life and his career on the line for people so unlike himself. Ironic but not insincere . . . or was he?

Bick helped Jess out of the car and brought her over to Juan Alvaro who met her halfway, with a gracious smile, a handshake, and one arm around his wife. Bick was still introducing them when Alvaro thanked Jess for driving his wife this long distance to her home. Jess had a mad impulse to blurt out the fact that she had been shanghaied into it, Alvaro being so famous for his honesty and directness. But she stifled her baser instincts and was polite, if not wildly enthusiastic.

"How very nice," she said. "You've been on my mind a great deal lately."

That made him laugh. Handsome, healthy teeth, she observed. Somehow, in spite of seeing him on television, she had supposed he must show signs of physical suffering, malnutrition, the hands of a laborer, something that explained his exploitation of the aching wounds of the migratory workers in this modern day. Her suspicion of his motives was given fuel by this puzzling inconsistency.

He answered her dubious, double-edged remark in his own way with something of her own husband's elegance, but she was aware that one or two people as yet unknown to her were still in the bungalow behind that screen door, listening and watching. She wondered if they could be reporters.

"Bick," she called, rudely interrupting Mr. Alvaro, "would you mind asking whoever is in there not to make this a political game? I came here because I enjoyed Mrs. Alvaro's company."

"Look here," Bick said striding toward the screen door, "I don't know anything about —"

Within the cool dark bungalow there was a movement, and it was Bick's sharp intake of breath rather than Jess's own recognition that made her stare at the face simpering at her through the screen.

What the devil was Mrs. Duvaux, of Duvaux Wines, doing here so cozily in the home of her family's worst enemy?

Jess found herself smiling one of those false, face-cracking wide smiles that she used at political rallies and cocktail parties for people she disliked but was forced to please for her husband's sake.

"How nice to see you," she began and added for insurance, "again!" The sight of short, squat Gladys Duvaux with her pinched but apparently happy round face, reminded Jess of something unpleasant — even dangerous — but the significance of this feeling escaped her. Besides, it was hard to feel anything very violent in the presence of a woman like Gladys Duvaux who was so determined to gush out her gossip and friendship.

"It isn't! But it is! This is an absolute miracle! Nothing but! Jessica, you've come in the nick of time to save me from falling under the spell of Elena's gorgeous husband. And you know how dear Chris would hate that. Come along in, Jessie."

Jessica hated the nickname Jessie and hadn't heard it in years, so that it was a perfectly natural angry face she turned to Mrs. Alvaro who, she saw at once, shared her contempt for Gladys Duvaux.

It was not until later when Jess had time to think, that it occurred to her Mrs. Alvaro's feeling toward the Duvaux woman was less contempt than puzzlement, and when this dawned on Jess, she wondered if even Mrs. Alvaro could understand the reason for Gladys Duvaux's visit and offered friendship. Surely this was a sign that the Duvauxs had come under, had agreed to whatever terms Alvaro imposed. Yet, Jess afterward remembered one uncomfortable thing about that afternoon gathering at the Juan Alvaro bungalow: the chilling atmosphere of suspicion.

Martinis and Manhattans were served, and Jess, glancing at the wine lady, had a notion the absence of wine was deliberate. It could have been merely the boycott Alvaro and his union had set in motion against the industry. But Mrs. Alvaro smiled and was extraordinarily pleasant to Gladys Duvaux, who, as far as Jess could see, merely hung about Juan Alvaro, honeying over him and a small, quiet, bookish man who, as Bick told Jess in a warning side-whisper, was Manny Caporetta, business manager for the field union. Except for the mystery that puzzled Jess — why was a Duvaux being so kind to an Alvaro, and vice versa? — she herself couldn't have cared less about Caporetta or Alvaro, she told herself. Nothing seemed half as intriguing to her as Mrs. Duvaux's presence here in the house of the enemy.

Just as Jessica was getting ready to leave,

half an hour after she had come — she was anxious to get home and report to Chris all she had seen and heard today — Gladys obligingly explained, "Darling, it's so absolutely marvy of you to show up here this afternoon. It only proves we've got into the right slipstream, so to speak. Peace. That's got charisma now. I'm the peace envoy between the wine industry and the workers. Aren't you with me?"

"Emphatically!" Jess said so firmly she got a quick, narrow-eyed look from the garrulous Gladys. "When do you start?"

"Oh, early. Dadda — that's my hubby, darling — he sent me here to wheedle darling Juan to a meeting — a nice, friendly sort of meeting, out here in the country . . . at a barbecue maybe. Anyway, he's agreed. And I adore his pretty wife. Though, frankly, I get the notion sometimes that she's afraid of us. Why on earth should she be scared of little old me?"

"Why, indeed?" Jess echoed and added the sarcastic rider, "Is there any reason why she should be?" She said this as she waved to the Alvaros across the cool, shadowy living room where they stood talking earnestly with Bick, while Caporetta, the business manager, tried to look as if he were not eavesdropping.

Gladys Duvaux pouted. "I don't think you heard me right, sweetie. I said they've not a thing to worry about. It's just that poor Juan's been so belligerent, making up all these awful stories about Mexicans we entice up here to starve before we hire them. Well, really! Did you ever?"

"Rarely," Jess said succinctly and went to the Alvaros to set down her cocktail glass and say good-bye.

Juan Alvaro looked at her with his steady gray eyes as he shook her hand.

"Please be understanding with your daughter, senator. I do not approve of children her age being out at all hours, picketing and otherwise involved in incitement to violence."

"I know," and the curious thing to Jess was that she meant it.

Alvaro smiled. "Thank you. I want you to know I try very hard to look out for the children who support us, like Miss March. I try to be certain they are never in the way of violence."

Jess surprised herself by saying suddenly, "The violence isn't of your making. It would be so much easier to fight you if it were." She turned away.

"Perhaps," he said as she joined Bick, "one day, your family will be united in our fight."

She waved to him, a tacit agreement, but

124

as she and Bick left the house, she remarked dryly, "That will be the day! Chris and Juan Alvaro on the same side."

After an odd little pause, Bick reminded her, "Chris isn't junior senator from California, *you* are. Juan may not be so very far off in his dreams after all."

That was a touchy subject, and she refused to go along with it. There was an ambivalence in the problem anyway. If Juan Alvaro and his union organizers were right, then they were actually against these poor devils she had seen around the wooden station wagon. And who could blame those eleven for yielding to the promises of pie in the sky made by the men who smuggled them across the border.

On the other side of the coin were the vineyard-owners and grape-growers, and the Wine Trust who claimed they could not afford to hire workers at legal wages. They did provide many of those migrant workers, smuggled in or not, with work, food, and salaries above those they received at home. She said this aloud to Bick as they made the approach to the bridge which would return Jess to the world she knew considerably better. Bick smiled.

"What about the people whose jobs they are taking? It's a little late for this country to glorify scab labor, isn't it? No matter how sympathetic they may be."

She knew neither he nor Mrs. Alvaro had intended that her sympathy for the eleven Mexicans around the beat-up station wagon should obsess her to the point of favoring these smuggled aliens instead of the thousands of American migrant workers currently deprived of jobs.

"That's what I get for playing a part," Jess muttered more to herself than to her companion. "I'm not senatorial material and never have been. The truth is, I'm sorry for both sides."

As they waited in line at the bridge tollbooth and Bick leaned over her to pay the toll, he was close to her face momentarily. Jess found her pulses pounding. With a sure instinct, she knew he shared that physical excitement. Was it only physical, that tie between them? She had always supposed the ties which first bound her to Chris March were far beyond the physical. For that reason she had made herself over into the image of what Chris wanted and expected. It was, surely, what she herself had wanted?

Yet now, she found herself so close to Bick's rough, tempting mouth she shivered with the effort not to yield to that temptation. Bick felt her retreat, though she hadn't moved. He said casually, "Sorry! Did I get in your way? Here goes, fella." He paid the toll and they moved ahead. Bick settled back beside her, pretending an extraordinary interest in the scenery of smoky industrial Richmond.

She let him off at his request at the Mac-Arthur Freeway, having exchanged hardly a dozen more words with him. She drove on up into the hills to the March home, to be met by Chris at the open doors of the garage, terribly upset, walking up and down the sloping driveway.

"Where the devil were you? Good Lord, Jess! I was getting ready to send out the bloodhounds."

Jessica was surprised to realize it was almost past the March cocktail hour. Her thoughts had been so chaotic, and often so painful, she remembered very little of the drive home. It really had been thoughtless of her, but the truth was, she had grown so used to living without Chris during the past months, and even years, that she often found herself forgetting about him entirely.

She drove on down the slope, into the garage. When she had cut the motor and was getting out, he came to hold the door open waiting sternly for her explanation. She put her hand in his and when he kissed her a little left of the mouth, but almost on target, she apologized, "I'm sorry, dear. A lot of things have happened since I left here this morning. I didn't notice the time."

Slightly mollified he explained as he walked her rapidly into the house arm in arm with her, "The Man told me he's going to mention me tonight on the news." He never referred to President Walters by name; it was always a cautious "he" or "The Man." "There's less than five minutes. Sue has everything set up around the TV in my den."

"The children?" she asked, trying to lash herself into the proper enthusiasm this event called for.

"Robin had some kind of doings in Berkeley and wanted to join those boys he rooms with — a bad influence on him. I've said it before, Jess. It really was a serious mistake when you let him fall in with them. He should never have been permitted to live away from home. Anyway, he stayed home and is in his room with Bethy."

She reminded him tartly in a way she would never have used before her illness, "He would have found it difficult to commute to Cal every day from Maryland!"

As Chris had chosen his own university for Robin, he realized he was on the losing side of the discussion and hastily amended, "Anyway, that's irrelevant now. The boy will be

128

home for dinner. He's waiting with Bethany at the TV in his own room, I believe. Hurry! We've got about a minute and a half."

Jess was amazed at how little all this mattered to her. Something besides the mere physical problem of her heart had happened to her since the attack. So many emotional matters had begun to have new meanings, new importance for her . . . that was what happened when you faced death, she supposed. Any ambition she might have had seemed to have faded, and worst of all, her ambition and pride in her husband, the center of her life, had begun to seem oddly inconsequential.

It was clear she wouldn't have time to wash or change. There was Walter Wingate frowning in his urbane way at the news in front of him, and saying something about President Walters being in fine fettle at a televised news conference today and Sue Lyburg, her blonde hair a bit askew, rustling around to get Jessica comfortable in a chair practically on top of the console television set. The girl looked at Chris half in exasperation, half in panic. Chris used to make me feel like that, thought Jessica.

"Oh, do hurry! You almost missed it!"

"My watch is slow," Chris complained. "This damned watch!"

Jess glanced at him. He seldom swore. But

then, he seldom had such crucial, life-and-death, emergencies as this!

Chris sat down hurriedly on the arm of Jessica's chair, resting one hand on the nape of her neck in the sensuous way that had always driven her wild in their early married days. He had often done this in public, the secret, highly erotic gestures that no one suspected, but which he knew were exceedingly effective with his wife. It was his own little joke, and since he was often less than effective in bed, she wondered if he was one of those men whose true life is lived in public and only his shadow life in private.

She looked up at him now, as his fingers moved on her neck, and he smiled down at her. For a breathtaking minute they were one again, as they had been the morning Robin was placed in her arms and Chris, leaning over the fuzzy-headed strange little mite, had whispered, "My own son. He'll carry on for me when I'm gone, thanks to my Jess, my love . . ."

Poor Chris! Robin hadn't quite carried on the way his father had pictured it. But then, his busy absentee parents had very probably been a disappointment to Robin as well. It was hard to know. He was not as decisive and positive and often wrong in his opinions, as his sister was.

"Sh!" Sue Lyburg cautioned the Marches, though no one had said a word.

President Walters, who rarely stood during question periods, sat at a long impressive mahogany desk, not his "work desk" as he called it, but the special setting when he answered newsmen's televised questions. He now jabbed a lean finger in the direction of someone at the back of the room. A loaded question about recent big-city riots was fired at him from Miss Corinne Curry whose middle-age spread and large-patterned clothing maligned the housewife image she projected. Miss Curry avoided kitchen stoves, nurseries and supermarkets like the plague, and got most of her exclusives late in the evening at a couple of elite cocktail bars, one in Washington and the other in a hush-hush but plush place in the hinterlands of Northern Virginia.

Chris cut into the president's answer which was firmly ambivalent to mutter to Jess, "They always take up time with this crap: same questions, same answers. Nobody dares tell the truth, what he'd really do about these damned riots."

Jessica glanced up at him curiously wondering what Chris would really do. He would not "send for the militia," "shoot to kill," or any other of the things he said in anger. He was much too cautious a man.

131

President Walters had answered a number of questions, mostly planted, to give him a chance for an easy airing of his views and plans. He had been swept in on a liberal and independent wave but was expected to conduct his office in a liberally conservative manner. "Voters don't always want what they ask for," was his true, if cynical observation.

Then came Miss Curry's planted question: "Mr. President, you are reported to have said the other morning that the American women might well decide the next election by their preference for or against the vice-presidential candidate. Would you care to elaborate on that?"

"Always glad to elaborate with the fair sex," said the President jovially, flashing his celebrated crooked smile which had been called "politically sexy."

"Sh!" whispered Sue Lyburg again. This time she encountered such a scowl from Jessica, her boss, that she blushed a little.

Someone enlarged on the question and President Walters, speaking as if he had never heard of a TelePrompTer, made the easy comment: "I read something the other day in the *Ladies' Home Journal* —" a row of titters and one or two guffaws interrupted him, and he grinned as if deliberately caught, "my *wife* read, the poll on the views of American women about their candidates. They want 'em moral, but not stuffy. They want 'em to have attractive wives who make a good help-mate. They want 'em good looking, young, healthy —" He paused.

"Sex appeal?" prompted one of the women reporters.

"But not too much," the president warned, making a wide spread-out gesture with both long arms.

There was a small furor as questions were shot at the president.

Jessica glanced at Chris; he was looking straight ahead, his beautifully tanned flesh pulled and tense, almost white. He cares *so* much! she thought, and wondered, not at his passion for office, but at her own total lack of interest.

President Walters came on loud and clear: "I agree. Very few who fit into that category." A tiny, careful pause, a pretense of thought, and the smile. "Well, there may be a few, besides Chris March, my Secretary of the Interior. On the other hand —" a shrug.

A Washington correspondent demanded sharply, "Will Chris March be your choice at the convention for your runningmate?"

The president looked surprised. "Did I say that? I'm sure there are many fine young fellows in our party. It just happened I couldn't recall anyone who fits that demanding job better than Secretary March . . . that's just off the top of my head, you understand."

The press all laughed. They understood very well how carefully each repetition of Chris March's name had been planted.

The president went on now to the international situation, the latest rocket booster, the trouble in the Middle East, and other trivia, as Chris remarked, turning away from the television set. Sue Lyburg got up and snapped the set off. For a brief, rebellious instant Jess thought of demanding that the set remain on, but realized the futility of it. Even she had no further interest in the press conference.

Almost at once the phones began to ring. Besides the numerous extensions, there were three lines, and all of them were busy. Jess knew what that was about. Everyone in the Bay area, plus points east and south, would be demanding to know what plans Chris had and whether he knew the president's plans.

The children still had the TV on, much too loud, in Robin's room and were discussing their own subject through the television voices. It made a noisy scramble. Jessica stuck her head in the doorway.

"Can you keep it down to a roar?"

"Oh, Mom!" That would be Bethy, but she

raised up from her cross-legged seat on the floor and would have lowered the television's volume if Robin hadn't beaten her to it.

Jessica's own phone was ringing in her room down the hall. She turned away saying, "Thanks, gang," thinking how odd it was to feel so tired when she had done very little all day but ride around. However, yesterday's visit to her doctors had been satisfactory, and the nurse was leaving soon. Her heart valves were all mending, or whatever they were supposed to do.

Suddenly she heard Bethany's shrill cry, "Louder, Rob! Get that!" and the television volume went up. There was a special bulletin cut into the regular news. Jessica, torn between the insistent ring of her telephone and the news bulletin, went back into Robin's room and stood behind the children.

The correspondent's dateline was San Francisco and he had already begun to speak. Bethy groaned, and Robin whispered, "Shut up!"

Jess caught scattered words before she understood the connection: ". . . at five-fifty-five. The explosion rocked the neighborhood of the small Alvaro home and the nearby Hot Baths. The car itself was —"

Jessica felt a roaring in her ears and stumbled tiredly to a hassock; her knees had given out. Robin put his arm around her, looking anxious, but poor Bethy was glued to the set and to the details of what appeared to be a gangland-type explosion in the wide cemented parking area of the Alvaro home.

Dazed, not yet feeling the real horror, Jess murmured, "I was there . . . only two hours ago . . . right there."

While the horrifying details went on, Bethy caught her mother's confused words and stared at her. "Mom, what are you talking about? You were *there* — at Mr. Alvaro's house?"

"Right there where it happened. Who — were there very many hurt?"

"Mrs. Alvaro and — of all people — Mrs. Duvaux, were cut by flying glass. Mr. Caporetta, the union business manager, was killed. He turned on the ignition of Mr. Alvaro's Ford in the driveway, and it — went boom." She shuddered.

Robin, who was watching Jessica closely, said, "Will you forget that damned business for a minute? Mother's sick."

This time Bethy's full attention was caught. She swung around on her knees beside Jessica, staring excitedly into her face.

"Mom!"

Jess was furious with herself. "Never mind me! Listen! It wasn't a dream! It was always *real,* and I was too stupid, or too blind —

or too *something* to know it was real!"

"Mom! Do you know what you're saying? You know something about this business?"

Jessica tried to think. It was horribly mixed up, and it went back to the day of her heart attack. There was the vagueness of it . . . had it all been some imagined talk, bits and pieces overheard in the street or among the reporters who interviewed her that morning, or whose meaning she had misinterpreted?

"I — think I know something, but I don't know yet quite what I do know. I've got to check back. I'll get Chris to help me go over everything I did that day." She got up hurriedly with new vigor. "Yes. I'll get Chris."

– EIGHT –

"Set it there," said Chris without looking up. "And keep it coming, good and hot. Plug the percolator over — oh! Jess. Are the children excited? Really rattles your back teeth, doesn't it?"

"What? The coffee?" The minute she came into the den, she was almost swept aside by the running back and forth of Sue and Mrs. Ryerson, the middle-aged nurse, who was a passionate partisan of the March political fortunes, at least the male March fortunes.

Chris looked up briefly, just the thread of a frown between his brows. Then he smiled and held out one hand. "Dear, we're all a bit nervous, but you mustn't take it out on me. Come here." She came slowly, hesitantly, realizing she would have a difficult time getting Chris to listen to a problem much more immediate than his political plans, but she came because for eighteen years she had come, delighting in being wanted by her idol, the idol of so many women.

"Hello, Jess, dear," he said in his quiet, well-modulated voice, as he drew her to him. He sat in his straight leather-cushioned "work chair," and although he must be quite as keyed-up as she, he was still able to be gentle and sweet to her now. She knew she should be deliriously happy. She looked down at him, mentally lashing herself to enthusiasm.

"My own phone is still ringing," was all she could think of in this moment of rare tenderness on his part.

He said, "Sue! Go Upstairs and take the senator's call, will you?"

Sue Lyburg flashed a puzzled glance at both the Marches. "Senator? But — oh. Mrs. — Senator March." And she hurried out.

Jess said dryly, "You should have specified which Senator March."

He shrugged. "The hired help these days!" He pretended to be suddenly roguish, masterful. "Bend down, woman! I want to kiss my wife, and I don't intend to move out of this comfortable chair."

She said, "Nothing could be less comfortable than that old chair," and secretly was horrified to find she didn't want to bend down to be kissed. Before she could carry out what very possibly was her first sexual resistance to him in her life, he evidently decided not to chance her refusal and pulled her, with his usual gentleness, onto his lap.

"Darling, aren't you feeling well? How's the old ticker?" He kissed her on the cheek, and his lips moved to her mouth, but she spoke, deliberately spoiling the carefully built-up mood.

"Chris, there's been a m-murder, and I think I know something about it."

"What?" He was so astonished he almost dropped her. "Jessica, have you been watching the late late show again?"

"I mean, I think I know about a clue. I may have heard some people — or a p-person who knew about it. I'd like to check back and see if I can remember." She was stammering, and it annoyed her. She must remember not to talk so fast, to think out every word first.

He began to laugh, and she felt his arms tighten their grip on her waist.

"Dear, a joke's a joke. But this —" He studied her face and must have read the hard, unswaying conviction he had never seen before. She had neither laughed when he did, nor had she broken down into that hesitant, feminine doubt that he could so easily conquer with quiet reason and firmness. "Jessica, if you could hear yourself! Better not let our distinguished Senator March go around talking about murders and clues, or they'd be getting out petitions at Fourteenth and Telegraph to recall my little girl."

He waited for what might have been a full

minute. It seemed longer to Jess. She said nothing, just looked at him. He raised one hand and gently pushed back a loose tendril of her sandy-gold hair, and in spite of herself she shivered with the old delight at his touch.

Seizing his advantage and correctly reading the meaning of that shiver, he went on smoothly, reasonably, "Now then, we'll shower and have dinner, and I'll finish the work this evening. Imagine! A whole campaign strategy, Jess. You'll feel better after all the excitement of the announcement wears off. As for you, my sweet girl, it's early to bed and a nice long night's rest for you."

"Chris?" she began and stopped.

He cocked a tawny eyebrow as he often did when asked the wrong question at a press conference.

"What? Mutiny in the ranks?" He was smiling, gentle and teasing. She had no real motive that she knew of for the appalling thing she said next.

"Not in the ranks, Chris. I've graduated. After all, *I* am the junior senator from California, not you. Remember?"

There was a clock ticking close by. Jess did not dare to turn and look. She sat there staring at a point in middle distance near the darkened television screen. She knew Chris well enough to understand how deeply she had cut him.

Apparently, however, there were worse things than the wound to him as her lover and her husband.

She tried to think of something, half explanation, half apology, anything that would gloss over her stupid reminder.

Then Chris looked around the room, shrugged, gave her his smile and patted her arm in a perfunctory way. He said with only a faint coolness, "I hope you aren't going to take that attitude in the campaign. After all, we are counting on Senator March to lead my California delegation."

I might have known. It all boils down to what's going to get Christopher March nominated!

He and Jess moved at the same time. She stood up, stunned, wondering what to do next. Chris looked around.

"Where the devil is that coffee? I've got a long evening ahead. I only hope the telephone lines hold out. There'll be plenty of wear and tear tonight. Will you have some coffee before you go upstairs, dear?"

"B-but, Chris! You haven't heard about the other business." She found herself stammering again. She had never stammered before the heart attack. It was something new coming on in moments of tension.

Now he was thoroughly in control again, picking up his black and gold telephone directory with one hand while he poured coffee with the other. He was too busy to glance her way.

"Some other time, Jessica. When you're feeling more yourself you can tell me all about the murders and the clues and the rest of it."

She turned away feeling stiff, angry, strong with her own deep, bitter knowledge. He got up, walked to the door and stared after her as she climbed the stairs.

"Jessica?"

She didn't look back, but she stopped. His voice trailed after her.

"Dear, please try to control that stammering when you are in public. It makes a bad impression."

The shock registered first, leaving her numb, and it wasn't until she reached her own rooms that the cruelty of the request hit her. She met Sue Lyburg coming out of the open door and ignored the girl's brusque explanation for the phone call she had taken: "Just more congratulations, Mrs. March — senator."

Jess closed the door and turned the lock sharply, emphatically. Then she went over, locked her dressing room door, and searched in the closet for the latest San Francisco telephone book. There was only the Oakland-East Bay book, of course. There would be a San

Francisco book downstairs in Chris's den, but that was out. She decided to call San Francisco information for Bick Haldean's number.

Almost immediately as she reached for it, the telephone began its busy ting-ting. She was angry enough not to answer but the telephone seemed likely to ring forever, so she took it up, listened to the appropriate congratulatory gush from someone named "Committee-woman Edna Case," and thanking her, cut off the connection, still with very little notion of the woman's identity and caring less.

She got Bickford Haldean's number at the Western Press Club and sat there on the bed feeling a belated stab of her husband's cruelty about the stammer. Never mind! she kept telling herself, more and more strongly. Bick will know what to do. Bick will care about murder. He will help me to remember what I heard, and most of all, whose voices I heard making the threats. I really did hear them, didn't I?

Bick was out, the club switchboard told her. He had gone out in a great hurry half an hour ago. There was no doubt where he had gone. Jessica gave her private number and left it at that. A few minutes later Bethy and Robin knocked on her door in a gingerly way and she got up and let them in.

"Mom, what's it all about?" the girl asked anxiously. "What did you mean? You knew about the explosion?"

Well, at least the children didn't think she was out of her mind!

She said, "I can't do anything tonight. I'll tell you more when I know more."

"But, Mom, if you *do* know something, it's your duty —"

Robin burst out angrily, "Leave her alone, Beth. Mother can handle whatever it is. No use in hounding her."

The girl turned on him. "And meanwhile, whoever did this will get away with it. What did you see, Mom? Where were you today?"

But Jessica's failure to reach Bick tonight had restored her to a degree of common sense. It would be idiotic for her to rush out into the night after a day of exertions and do — she didn't know what. Somewhere in her hazy memory of that day of the heart attack, there was Gladys Duvaux's voice, for instance. But had Gladys actually known anything about a plot to assassinate Juan Alvaro, or had she merely expressed a fervent, thoughtless wish for his death?

Somewhere that day, there was a sentence or two, a voice, maybe more than one, suggesting a clear foreknowledge of the assassination plot. The question was: whose voice? How many were in the plot, if there was one, and who was to be hired as the killer? Even the identity of the actual killer was not so important as the identities of those who hired him.

Jessica said calmly, "I'm going to bathe and have my dinner in bed, I'm going to get some sleep, and then tomorrow when I feel fresh, I'm going across the Bay on a — shopping expedition."

"Mom! Shopping? When people are being murdered under our noses?"

But in spite of Bethany's public-minded indignation and Robin's insistence that they would eat with her, Jessica remained firm. When the children had gone, she knew she had crossed the Rubicon. Senator Jessica March, the shadow-senator, ventriloquist Chris March's dummy, was a changed woman. The complex she had felt for too many years, and which was carefully nourished by Chris — her inadequacy, his own graciousness in marrying Jess Souza, the nobody — had been blown wide open and shown up in all its phoniness.

He needs me more than I'll ever again need him.

After her bath and a light dinner served with flair by Robin, supported by his sister who spent her time in outraged comments on the Alvaro assassination attempt, Jessica lay thoughtfully in bed watching the news bulletins. These alternated between Alvaro

146

reports and proud interviews by Californians, frequently the man in the street, on the subject of their own ex-Senator, Chris March, being most-likely candidate for the vice-presidential nomination.

Late in the evening after Jess had dozed briefly came an interview with handsome, toothy Dexter Dominik. She had awakened suddenly to the sound of his unctious voice and thought with a certain ironic amusement, three cheers for Chris March, boy vice-president! She knew it was unfair to castigate poor Chris for being the man he always had been, but all the things she thought of as threatening to their marriage seemed to be epitomized by D.D. and his perpetual-motion politics.

At least, in the old days, she could look forward to week-end picnics with Chris and the children up in the Oakland Hills and, later in his career, walks in the Virginia woods. The quiet evenings at the Maryland house were too often interrupted by noisy political cocktail parties with the air smudged by bourbon and tobacco and irritating voices.

Suddenly she sat up to listen. The interview had taken a different and more urgent turn.

D.D. said suddenly, "But of course, Chris March's thoughts tonight are on something far closer to his heart than his possible inclusion on the ticket. His first concern is, and always has been, the welfare of his first friends, the migrant workers in California's many industries. Even though Senator March — I should say Secretary March — felt that Mr. Alvaro was being used by out-of-state influences, they have always remained good friends. This business of the attempt on Mr. Alvaro's life — the death of Manny Caporetta, Mr. Alvaro's business agent — that's what's on everyone's mind tonight. Chris March, at this minute, is in the process of demanding an investigation into this hideous crime. And as you know, Chris March gets results!"

This brought on a spate of sympathetic references to the Alvaros, and the information which Jessica was exceedingly happy to hear, that there were no other serious injuries in the explosion. Alvaro had gone back to the house for his briefcase just before Caporetta started the car, and the two women, Mrs. Alvaro and Mrs. Duvaux, sustained only minor cuts and scratches from the flying glass.

When the news bulletins had been cleared, it was back to the nightly movies and the variety shows. Jessica snapped off the remote-control button and then the bed lamp. In spite of the many thoughts running through her head, she felt sure of herself and her position which, in spite of all D.D.'s smooth talk, was probably against that of Chris. She cared very much what happened to the Alvaros — and she was fairly sure Chris could not care less.

It shook her, therefore, to hear Chris's footsteps outside her door shortly after her light went out. Usually when she heard this, she called to him almost before he opened the door. Tonight, she felt a new and rather ghastly reluctance to have him come to her. He tried the door which Robin had left unlocked, and then stuck his head in. The light from the hall glinted on his tawny hair and she thought again, as a thousand times before, how handsome was that head of his! And yet, at sight of it, she was moved only by astonishment at her own indifference to the sight of it.

"Jess, darling? Are you asleep yet?"

There was an awkward minute before she answered, "No."

He closed the door behind him and came in, tiptoeing as in a sick room, making his way to her bedside with the help of the light through the thin drapes at the wide southerly windows.

"Feeling better, sweetheart?"

She saw that he was in pajama bottoms as he always was when he came to her, his upper body splendidly bare, the jacket over his arm. It seemed remarkable to her, how much a man of habit he was. Did he never get bored with doing things the same way? Even the streets he traveled, the way he made love? She wondered if a person used rigid habits to conceal some feeling of inadequacy, an insecurity she had never suspected.

"I can't be feeling better. I wasn't sick tonight."

He got into bed beside her and then surprised her by touching his lips to her exposed shoulder. That, at least, was not in his usual pattern. There were fumblings on his part under cover of darkness, adjusting his pajamas — did he do that also according to rote? — and then he murmured close to her ear, "But we musn't forget, you've been a very sick girl. It's no wonder my little girl was talking wildly about clues and late late shows. Heart attacks are no laughing matter."

She reminded him with grim satisfaction, "Don't be silly. It was nervous exhaustion."

"Darling —" he began, trying to curb his growing impatience.

But she reminded him, "You know it's true. Didn't President Walters say so?"

"Never mind President Walters. Darling, you're giving me the cold shoulder. Turn around to your old man."

He hadn't called her that since he won his first Congressional election. She turned over and faced him, let his hands roam over her bare shoulder and then under the chiffon shoulder strap and over the warm, soft flesh of her breast. In spite of her anger, her determination not to yield to the old desire for him, the flesh of her breasts hardened and peaked under the practiced, almost mechanical movements of his hand.

After that, she was captive to whatever desires he chose to satisfy upon her body, as she always had been. And after he rapidly finished, he left her bed, with the final reward to her: "I'm sorry, Jess, about the stammering thing. I know you've been under a strain. Dr. Cherin tells me it often happens to people after periods of great stress, so —" he patted her hip companionably, "my little girl must not let herself worry about things. Just go along, roll with the punches, as they say. Don't get too involved."

"I am involved," she returned sharply. "With an assassination."

He sighed, an impatient noise that used to terrify her by its suggestion of his haughty disapproval. "Good God, Jessica! Don't start that again."

At the door he turned and snapped on the light. It blinded her momentarily and she could hardly make out his face and figure, but of one thing she was sure: he was coldly angry.

"If you've been listening to Bethany with her babble about the Alvaro affair, I want you to stop it! This whole business is dangerous."

"Dangerous?" She sat up. "You mean — to us?"

"Certainly. Sympathy for him could easily give his whole movement a national importance. They know I'm against his rabble-rousers. It could cost me the nomination."

"Oh," she slid back under the covers, "that kind of danger." I might have known, she told herself. . . .

Shortly before eight the next morning the telephone rang. Jessica had taken her pills and gotten a good night's sleep in spite of her busy thoughts. She was stepping out of the shower when she heard the phone. She hurried to answer it in her wet terry cloth robe and was delighted to hear Bick's dear, warm, excited voice.

"Jess? You all right? Christ! Your message gave me a jolt. I just got in. I've been up-country on the Alvaro business."

"But then you've been up all night! You must be dead for sleep," she apologized, and then at his denial, his obvious anxiousness to be of help to her, she explained briefly, "I've got to see you. I need your advice. It's — it may be a matter of life and death."

"Sounds intriguing. If so, I'm your man

. . . but then, I always have been." He stopped, and just before the pause could be embarrassing, he added lightly, "And you'd have known it if you hadn't been so damned ambitious to be a governor's wife, and whatnot."

"I've gone way beyond that now. In fact, I'm headed for the what-nots. Bick, where can I see you? And when?"

"Had breakfast?"

"Not yet."

"Good. Meet me at the London Room. I've got a corner there that they keep sort of private for me. How soon?"

She had been counting up the minutes it would take to dress, make up, get the car out, fight the bridge traffic . . .

They agreed on the earliest possible minute of meeting, and she set the phone back and began to dress hurriedly, playing down her usual expensive-conservative look, trying to blur her identity. She drank orange juice and a cup of Sanka to give her the energy to fight the bridge traffic and left a note for Chris, saying she was going to see a Marchers for March club in the city. This was true enough, inversely. It was at a Marchers Club, she thought, that the talk about assassinating Alvaro had begun for her.

She went quietly down the back stairs to

the garage, hearing Chris's electric portable typewriter going rapidly and guessed he had spent his night making dream-plans for the future. She found herself envying him the simple straight line of his mental and emotional drive. Surely nothing could stop such a man!

She drove to San Francisco obsessed by her own single ambition to track down that lost day in her life and, in doing so, uncover whatever could be known of a plot to assassinate Juan Alvaro. Bick met her at an unobtrusive side entrance of the hotel which housed the London Room. No one either saw or noticed them, for which she was profoundly grateful. When Bick took her hands between his big ones, she seemed to absorb some of his strength and the vigor of his personality as they walked down the thickly carpeted steps to a lower-level corridor. Thanks to the hilly aspect of the city, this lower level ended a block away in the ground-floor lobby of the hotel.

Fortunately it was not necessary for Bick and Jessica to cross the main lobby to reach the London Room. The lobby at that hour was full of members to an AFL convention, and considering the present March ambivalence on the subject, Jess had no anxiety to be cornered by them and pinned down for a quote. Bick took Jess into the dark, comfortable, timbered room and received a knowing nod from the head waitress who glanced toward a banquette in a shadowed corner.

Jess got a jolt when she saw a short, dark, resolute-looking man get up from the banquette to meet them. Bick said, "I thought Pete could help us. Senator Jessica March, Pietro Tognazzi. Pete does a little labor investigative work."

It made her nervous to be describing half-remembered sounds to a stranger who probably held the melodramatic title of undercover man. Such suspicions could have frightful effects and would spread endlessly. Jess March's own involvement, even if her suspicions proved groundless, might react against Chris in some way.

She sat down between the two men, her manner cold, her whole excitement about these dreams and voices of hers, suddenly crushed by the presence of an outsider, someone she couldn't trust. She said so aloud.

"Bick, this was extremely confidential. It's only a suspicion of mine. Something I overheard. Or thought I overheard. I'm sure you understand, Mr. Tognazzi."

The hard-faced little man did not smile or make smooth denials. He glanced across the table at Bick who shrugged. Tognazzi cleared his throat. He had an exceptionally quiet but powerful voice.

"Sure, senator. I know how you feel. But there's a few things you have to consider. I've been telling Haldean here the possibilities. There's going to be talk pretty soon. It's starting already."

Jessica caught her breath. "But I haven't said a word. Outside my own family no one but Bick knows. It would be terrible to accuse somebody like Gladys Duvaux or the others with no more proof than something I hardly remember hearing."

"You don't understand, Jess." Bick covered her hand briefly and she looked at him, puzzled and more uncomfortable than ever. "Pete is trying to tell you that what happened yesterday is going to be used — not by Alvaro, but by his enemies. They're already spreading the story that Alvaro had quarreled with his union business manager, the man who died."

Jess looked at the two men, baffled by what appeared to be a fantastic notion.

"They must be crazy! Why would Alvaro take such a chance? Surely any idiot can see where a story like that would come from! To cover their own tracks."

Bick reminded her with a whimsical little smile, "Now, honey, you know why it's so important that we track down the identities of those women you heard that day."

She tried to fight the rising panic.

"Track down? I don't even know for certain that I heard anything. I was sick that day. I may have imagined the whole thing!"

"You'd better not have imagined it, senator," said the short dark man. "You'd really better not."

- NINE -

"Look here!" she began angrily, both resentful and frightened at being used. She lacked the highly developed sense of drama that made men like Chris and even Bick Haldean enjoy being in the limelight, the very focal point of that drama. This lack in her had made the role of senator doubly difficult. She felt that same lack, the same resentment now. "I told Bick I thought I heard some women talking. That's all it amounts to. I was in the process of having a heart attack. No one in his right mind could use this as evidence." She pulled her hand out from under Bick's and frowned at him. "Use your head, Bick. You know that. Tell him exactly what I told you on the phone."

"Sorry, senator." The dark man cut in. "I think I already got the full details from Bick. We know how bad you were feeling, but you heard half a dozen women talking about getting rid of Alvaro. Women whose husbands — every one of them — had good reason to hate Alvaro and want him out of the way. Even the idea that you *think* you heard something is important. You had no reason to conjure it up, out of a clear sky so to speak."

"I don't see why it's important. After all, my sympathies, in some ways, are with the Alvaros, and since I was surrounded by his enemies, and was feeling rotten, I could easily have imagined I heard those voices against him."

Bick put in quickly, "Were your sympathies with the Alvaros that day?"

Her head had begun to ache with all this pulling and hauling, but Bick's reminder seemed to pierce the darkness of her confusion. She exclaimed impatiently, "No. I hadn't thought of that. How stupid! You're right. I wasn't thinking about Alvaro. I just heard him being talked about."

"Well then!" Pete Tognazzi opened his short muscular hands briskly with satisfaction. "That's it!"

"But it's so vague — just voices," she protested, rubbing her forehead anxiously. "I'm pretty sure it wasn't in my suite. It happened at the Gold Room Bar, beyond that wall behind you. I'm going in there when we leave here. See if I can relive the whole scene." The two men stared at her and then at each other. She added with a faint effort at humor, "It always worked with Charlie Chan on the late late show."

They both laughed. Bick slapped her on the

back with a pretense of gusto. "Okay. As soon as I get you to eat something. Charlie Chan was a stout fella, you know. Here's the girl. What are you going to have?"

She ordered chipped beef on toast and both men ordered eggs Benedict. While they were eating they tried to make small talk with each other and with Jessica but she had a very strong feeling that beneath all the banter, they were as anxious and as nervous as she was over the possible results of Jessica's re-enacting that famous cocktail hour with the Lady Marchers.

It seemed a very long time, but actually they had hardly eaten anything when Pete Tognazzi pushing his half-full plate back, said, "We all ready to go at it?"

Jessica had eaten little of her own excellent meal, though she made an elaborate pretense pushing bits of now soggy toast around her plate with her fork. She knew by the flutter of something inside her — heart? nerves? — that she was all keyed up for that visit to the Gold Room to play at being Charlie Chan. She was too nervous or too uneasy to think it was funny when Bick said, "We've got to update you, Jess, from Charlie Chan to James Bond."

As they were getting up, Pete Tognazzi asked suddenly, "What does your husband

160

think of this business?"

Jessica looked around just in time to see Bick's quick, chopping gesture behind her back. He was clearly telling his friend Tognazzi not to pursue the subject of Jessica's husband. The gesture came too late.

"My husband is extremely interested in apprehending the murderer — whoever he is."

She thought Tognazzi hesitated just a shade before he agreed in a surprisingly smooth voice, "Naturally . . . the proper attitude in every way. Shall we go?" He stepped aside with such a blatant effort to rush her that she almost decided to renege and give up playing detective. It seemed to her that Tognazzi's whole attitude clearly was aimed at knocking Chris in some way. She resented it with all the passionate wifely loyalty built up through eighteen years of living with and for Chris.

But when she moved out of the banquette and started to crush the two men with her refusal to cooperate, she knew she had to go on with it. "All right. We're off to the Gold Room. But you stand the drinks. Okay?"

"Right, Charlie," Bick promised her as he dropped bills on the check at the table and took her arm.

Pete Tognazzi walked on her other side and though she joked with them as they left the London Room, she was wondering

161

what would happen if she couldn't remember anything once they reached the cocktail lounge. The men were counting too much on something that had been vague and confusing at best.

Surprisingly enough for this early hour there were a number of people in the bar when the Charlie Chan threesome walked in. Jess didn't recognize any of the bar's habitués, but then the bar was its usual dimly lit self. Her first reaction was something like seasickness, a queasy feeling engendered by memories of her other illness that must have begun in here, and also the faint but inescapable smell of bourbon everywhere.

She reached into the outside pocket of her handbag and took out the white linen handkerchief which she usually carried merely as a crisp, clean note to her costume. This time, she put the handkerchief to her nose. Bick looked at her. He seemed a little worried, which was not surprising under the circumstances.

"The whiskey smell," she explained. "At this hour of the morning, it makes my stomach turn over."

Tognazzi had begun to move around the room aimlessly, doubtless hoping to find some suggestion of a clue, to reproduce the atmosphere of that preluncheon cocktail party with its ominous undertones. Bick leaned on the darkly gleaming bar and watched Jessica as she closed her eyes relying now on her other senses to recreate the scene.

"Are you okay, honey?" he asked when she shook her head, as if angry at herself.

"I'm fine, or would be if I could clear the air of that infernal whiskey smell." She smiled at Bick, moving closer to him. "It's funny, but my most evocative sense — the one that always brings back my childhood memories — is my sense of smell — my nose. It's infallible."

He studied her fingers thoughtfully, then took them in his hand and held them a minute, as if to protect them from the world's dangers. But a part of his mind was actively engaged on the subject of the long-gone cocktail party.

"We'd better order something, I think," he said finally, when the stare of the barman became unavoidable.

She laughed and wrinkled her nose. "It's true the whiskey smell is smothering my memories, but there's something I hate even worse: a Duvaux fizz. It's made with —"

"Don't tell me — the wine of our friend Gladys."

"Ghastly stuff. I had one — a fizz, I mean — that day of my heart attack. The whole place was full of them. I nearly got

163

lynched when I ordered a martini. That awful smell of sour wine permeated the —"

They stared at each other. With one voice they whispered excitedly, "That's it!"

Bick turned to the barman. "Give us two Duvaux fizzes."

The barman rolled his eyes but went to work. When Pete Tognazzi saw what was going on he returned to the bar just as the two glasses of bubbling white wine were set before Jessica and Bick.

"What's all this? Doesn't look very appetizng."

"Never mind that," Bick told him abruptly. "Order a Duvaux fizz and stand behind Senator March. We're trying out an experiment in evocation via smell."

"Evo — what by *what?*"

When it was explained to the investigator he grinned and agreed, with the added proviso, "I don't have to drink it, do I?"

He was reassured but upon receiving his glass he took his place behind Jessica and raised the glass to his mouth, muttering, "The things I do for Union Labor!"

The sour taste of wine at this time of the morning was sickening to Jessica as well, but then it had been sickening to her on that other occasion, when the "Marchers" had filled the room with their shrill chattering voices and the strong odor of Duvaux fizzes. She sipped the wine and found herself sniffing the air at the same time. Nothing came to her, no sudden clue or earth-shaking sensation that she had lived this moment before. She said finally over her still-brimming glass, "It's no use. Nothing seems to come to me. I feel like a medium without her Indian guide." She sipped a little and at the same time sensed something she had been searching for, that groping for the instant which was suddenly here.

"Over behind you," she said loudly, startling her two companions. She saw their reaction and lowered her voice but closed her eyes again, the better to siphon all her senses into that one sense so powerful in her, the sense of smell: "She mentioned the word first — assassinate — something about how they always assassinate the wrong man. I thought she was talking about the Kennedy assassination in Los Angeles. Then someone hushed her up. 'Puddles,' they called her."

"Puddles," Pete Tognazzi repeated slowly. Jess opened her eyes and stared at him but couldn't tell whether he recognized the nickname or not.

"Go on," Bick prompted her.

She closed her eyes and sipped the wine. By recalling *Puddles* and *assassination,* she moved on a bit in memory. "I didn't realize it then. It was later. It seems to me, though, that there was a deep voice, deeper than the others . . . something about getting rid of competition . . ."

"What didn't you realize?"

"The full implications. That it was murder they were talking about." She opened her eyes and looked at the two men, her senses sharpened now. "Until we went into the Gold Ballroom! That was when I knew! Some woman was chattering away in my ear and I felt miserable. I wanted her to stop making noises, give me some peace and quiet."

"It was a woman. You're sure of that?" asked Tognazzi. His voice was rougher. The suspense and the chance of a failure to discover anything concrete were obviously wearing on his nerves. Jess felt she had failed both men. She would never provide them with even the small clue to start them on the often difficult road to pinning down an assassin — or a group of assassins?

"That time, in the ballroom —" She moved over to the huge, paneled doors that shut in the Gold Ballroom. She tried the old-fashioned latch with her free hand. It moved under her pressure, and she looked into the long, empty room with its closed-in smell. She felt that she had done all this before, the furtive peeking into the room, the feeling of bravery and daring, but the other time, she and her father had danced the length of the ballroom before being thrown out. She studied the shadowy recesses of the room and the opposite side across from the doors, where the speakers' table had been set up and heard again the chattery female:

"He deserves what he gets . . . I don't know all the facts," or something like that, "and I don't care about knowing them."

And then Jessica's realization that this, following on such remarks as she had heard in the bar — "not murder, merely eliminating the competition" — meant there was a plot to assassinate someone and the most likely candidate was Juan Alvaro.

She turned around and almost walked into Bick. He took her by the shoulders, startling her by his intense and worried expression. "Honey, all this isn't too much for you?"

She found it ridiculous, yet curiously comforting that he cared that much about her rather than the business at hand. It was something she was not used to. And yet, Bick had always been this way, even in the early days when they were both young . . . younger, she amended, for she suddenly felt very young now, glowing under his masculine, protective care of her.

"I've never felt better in my life, Bick. Never." She moved her head and with a quick gesture that surprised them both, she touched her lips to his hand.

Pete Tognazzi's voice, louder than usual, cut away the tenderness of those few seconds: "Well, what's the answer? Is that all you remember?"

"Lower your voice, for God's sake!" Bick muttered much more angrily than the interruption warranted.

Pete looked over his shoulder, but nobody seemed interested in them, except the barman who was almost excessively busy polishing the bar at a point nearest them.

"Sorry. Anyway we've got a couple of things to go on. Best thing is that nickname — Puddles."

Bick took Jessica's arm and said with a slight tilt of the head toward the barman, "Let's get out of here."

They left then, returning to the street by the corridor, the longer but less-crowded way than the nearby main lobby. There was no one around when they stopped at the street door.

"You kids run along," Tognazzi said. "I'm going to smell out what I can upcountry." He had one hand in his coat pocket and the other on his tie. "You still sure you don't know who

Puddles is?" He was very close to Jessica.

Bick said suddenly, "For Christ's sake, Pete, you don't have to breathe down our necks!"

Since the man was clearly all business, Jessica couldn't figure out what Bick was angry about until she glanced at Tognazzi's bulging pocket and then at his peculiar interest in his own tie. Belatedly she understood.

"You've been r-recording everything I've said!" And Bick had known all about it. It was a rotten trick, even if she had been the housewife she would like to be. In the circumstances, as a U.S. Senator, she knew the great danger of having her words taped. They might be used out of context, made into a weapon against her by Chris's political enemies.

Pete Tognazzi started to say something, reddened, and looked at Bick. "She's got no reason to trust me. You tell her she can rely on me."

Jessica was already fumbling to free herself from Bick's clasp but he shook her a little, not ungently.

"Listen, Jess! This guy plays his little tapes over and over to himself. He gets his best ideas that way. He figures out things. You do want him to get to the bottom of this, don't you?"

Her anger was building every second. "It's

169

a dirty, foul trick! You know how dangerous tapes can be, particularly in an election year. You could t-twist around what I said until I confessed to the murder myself!"

They were stalemated.

"Give it to her," Bick said finally.

Tognazzi shrugged, took the little recorder out of his pocket, and snapped out the cartridge. He handed it to her and Jessica reached out for it. At the same time, she thought of the bomb that destroyed the union business agent on a spot where she herself had been standing only a couple of hours before . . . and she thought of Chris March's total lack of interest in the crime.

"Go ahead," she said suddenly. "If Bick says you're all right, take it."

When she and Bick were out on the street and walking to the garage under Union Square, he apologized again about the taping of the interview pointing out, "I was against it. I knew you just wanted to do a run through of your ideas about that day, the scattered remarks you remembered. But there was always the chance that you'd forget some seemingly unimportant detail later. This way, it's all there for us to work on. And if you think of anything else, we can add that."

Now that she had made up her mind, she didn't want to talk about the tape, but about the implications of what she remembered.

"I know it's not evidence in itself. But doesn't it give us an inkling that there really was an assassination planned by one of the growers, as opposed to this lie they're spreading that Alvaro planned it himself?"

"It's absolutely the *only* argument on our side, or let's say, on the side of truth. I'll be keeping in touch with Pete now that we're sure there really was a plot, Jess." He looked down at her in that special way of his. He didn't smile, but the warmth in his eyes seemed to assure her that he was happy in her company.

They started down the ramp into the garage and heard a ringing girlish voice cry, "Hi, Bick!" which echoed and reechoed through the caverns of the garage.

"Good Lord!" Jess swung around hastily. "That's Bethany's voice." There was nothing wrong with Bethy's finding her mother here in San Francisco. The note Jess had left clearly said she was going to a Marchers gathering, but she still had the uneasy feeling that her own daughter might consider her a rival for Bick's attentions — a shocking rival, considering her married state. No matter how unsettled Jessica's home life might be, she knew it could not excuse the emotion she sensed between Bick and herself.

171

"Why do you jump like that?" Bick asked her in an impatient voice. "Are you afraid of young Beth?"

It was impossible to tell him that one of her fears involved her own daughter's jealousy. But there was an overriding fear, greater than the rest.

"I said something to her last night about having been at the Alvaros. Now she's here in town. I don't want her mixed up in it. You know how dangerous that could be. She's so impulsive."

"Like you, Jess?"

She was looking down the ramp and then back up behind them to the street. Bethany came clip-clopping around the doorway in Mexican sandals and down the ramp after them.

"Mom! What are you doing here? Bick, you've got to help her. Dad's no good for a job like this. He couldn't care less."

Bick watched them as Bethy hugged her mother, and Jess caught the quick, then vanishing look on his face that told her a poignant story of Bick's own need: the necessity to belong. She thought it possible that the hardened bachelor envied the marriage which produced this normal devotion between mother and daughter.

"Come on. Tell me the truth," Bethy

wheedled the two of them, pulling Bick into the little group. "You are doing some police work. Mom knows something to do with poor Mr. Alvaro, and you're helping her."

"Shut up, kid," Bick told her brusquely, but he leavened it with a smile.

"Oh! I get it. Undercover stuff." Bethy looked at him. "Bick, I came into the city to see if I could do something. I know you'll help the Alvaros."

"You can't do a thing, kid, except take your mother back home — and say nothing."

"Don't call me kid!" Bethy demanded, but she added, "Whatever you say, Bick. Mom? He's wonderful isn't he — my friend Bick? Look at him blush!"

Jess did not look at him as she agreed quickly, "Yes, yes. He's wonderful. Would you mind driving me home, dear? Somebody can pick up your car later." She had a nasty prickle of fear along her spine which warned her that Bethy might be in some kind of danger if she hung around San Francisco talking about murder and secrets. Whatever was in back of the recent murder at the Alvaro house, Jessica was fairly sure it involved more than the actual assassin who set the dynamite mechanism to go off when the driver of the Ford turned the key in the ignition. This was a conspiracy, and now that Jess had done her part, the Marches were better off at home; let the professionals take it from here.

The two women said good-bye to Bick, got Jessica's car and drove out of the garage. Just as they pulled out on the street, Jess saw dark little Pete Tognazzi hustling toward the garage. She asked Bethy to stop and called to him. He was breathless when he reached the car.

"Bick down there, senator?"

"A little behind us. Have you found something?"

"I know who Puddles is!"

Bethy looked past her mother's head at Pete, but she was intelligent enough to say nothing.

"Marvelous! Who is she?" Jess asked.

"Dame named Pudney-Clormann. Husband's the new general manager of Croisetti Farms."

Jess slapped the car door with one gloved hand.

"Then that proves I didn't imagine all that! I really heard it. This Clormann woman *must* know something."

Pete Tognazzi sighed. "Yeah. She must, all right. My informants tell me she had left the Bay area the day before for Europe. Davos, Switzerland, I think. She's still there, incidentally."

"Ridiculous! I couldn't have made up the name, since there really is a Puddles. They're trying to cover up." He nodded, and she began to see other unpleasant phases to this investigation. "How do they know? I mean — did they just have this story ready, or have they got long ears? How did they know you were going to check on Puddles, of all people?"

"Their ears aren't too long, just active. The barman in the Gold Room went on his relief the second we left there. I'm told he made a phone call."

Jess shivered. Then she looked into the rear-view mirror.

"Bick's coming. By God! I hope you nail them dead to rights! Let's go, Bethy."

Bethy did as she was told. She might be impulsive, but she could be surprisingly mature in a crisis. Bethy's silence now gave Jess time to think, and what she thought made her sick with disgust at the things she and Chris had been blind to. If Chris were ever made aware of the murky background to the whole affair of the laborers and growers, he must find some compromise. But he was so deaf whenever anything intruded on his immediate plans!

"Sometimes I wonder," she mused aloud as they drove onto the Bay Bridge ramp.

"Wonder about what, Mom?"

"Well, your father is so ambitious. He won't let anything get in his way. Why on earth did he commit that one, single, unambitious act? Why did he marry Jess Souza?" She laughed a little to show she was half joking.

The awkward thing was Bethy's unexpected reaction. She raised her head sharply and gave her mother a furtive sidelong glance. She did not laugh. A minute or two later she said, "This damn traffic! Makes me dizzy!"

It was almost as if she knew the answer to that silly, and almost-rhetorical question. Why had Chris March, the ambitious, married Jess? It was odd, and troubling, Bethy's manner.

– TEN –

They had reached the Oakland turnoff before Bethy said, after what appeared to be a great deal of thought, "You know, Mom, you probably think Bick Haldean is like an old shoe or something. You've known him since time began and —"

"Only since I was your age," Jess reminded her.

"Yes. Well, anyway," Bethy brushed off trivialities, "he's being positively budgy about it all. He treats me like — you know — like he had to make a daily four-carbon report to my Mom."

"I know." Jessica avoided her daughter's eyes and stared out of the car window. In the distance, piercing the low layer of smog over the east bay was the slender campanile of the University of California, and she wondered if Robin would be going back there in the fall. Or would that too have to be sacrificed because, although it had produced more Nobel Prize winners than any other university in the world, it did not now fit precisely into Chris March's image of himself and his family?

Beth pursued her subject stubbornly. "I

177

wish you'd do me a favor, Mom. Couldn't you give Bick a hint — you know — tell him you're not going into spasms just because he's a little bit older than me."

That jarred Jessica out of her painful thoughts. "A *little* bit!"

"You know what I mean. I'm mature for my age, and he's awfully young for his. All the gang say so. They say he really is onto our wavelength. So it isn't as impossible as you think."

"I never said it was impossible."

"Well you certainly act funny. You simply can't hold a grudge against him after all these years, just because he ditched you or had another girl, or whatever happened all those ages ago."

"You make me feel like Methuselah."

"Oh, Mom."

Jessica sighed and took a shallow, nervous breath. "What were you thinking of a while ago when I was talking about your father marrying me?"

"What was I thinking? Oh, Mom, you're so silly! I was thinking what anybody would, that Daddy doesn't deserve you."

Perversely this annoyed Jess, and she was more abrupt than she intended to be. "Don't talk like that. You don't know —" she laughed, with a sudden memory, "you can't

178

imagine what a job it was, between your grandmother and your father, to educate me into my place as his wife. I was just a gauche, half-educated . . . kid. And I knew it. Your Daddy has always been very good to me."

"I know. He never beat you or chased around much, or drank. But — he's the most selfish person in the whole world. Even Grandma's not that selfish." Bethy flashed dimples in a smile. "I think I'm a little bit like Grandma Augusta in some ways."

"Bethy, your passion for justice and your interest in these migratory workers, aren't they a little like your father's passion to be vice-president? Wouldn't you sacrifice almost anything for these causes of yours?"

"I'm not as wrapped up in myself as Daddy is. I mean, I care about these people as well as my own ambition."

"So does your father."

Bethy said nothing to that, but her very nice lips were suddenly thin, severe. She looked like her father when he was upset; it aged her considerably.

"Okay. Have it your way. I've just got one thing to say. Grandma told me something last year in Maryland. I was all up a loop about some cause in Baltimore: black kids that couldn't go to my school. And Grandma said I was just like my mother.

179

If I wasn't careful, she said, my folks would have to buy *me* a husband."

Jessica baffled both Bethany and herself by bursting into laughter, hearty enough not to be hysterical. "That's the funniest thing I've heard in eighteen years. No, really, *the* funniest! Augusta must have finally flipped that expensive wig of hers! *Me buy Chris March!* With what? That's gorgeous! Absolutely the end!"

They avoided the subject after that, and reached home in what, to Jessica, was an unnatural stillness. It was not often that Bethany was thrown, conversationally. Jess suspected the girl still believed Augusta's fantastic lie, and she couldn't understand why. Bethy was an intelligent girl, and more than that. She was seldom fooled by Augusta's aristocratic pretenses, or her occasional needling remarks. What was back of it all?

She found Chris walking up and down the long formal regency living room whose drapes were securely closed. He, like her recent acquaintance, Pete Tognazzi, was armed with a tape recorder, and was making a speech into a discreet, professional-looking microphone. He looked around as Jessica came in, nodded and smiled to acknowledge her presence, but kept on with his speech. She recognized it as one he would probably be delivering to the national committee heads in Philadelphia in two weeks. It sounded good, urbane, conciliatory, seeing civil rights in particular a matter for accommodation on both sides.

She sat down on the edge of an uncomfortable tapestry chair nearby and listened to him finish the speech. She was impressed as always by his manner, his excellent, well-modulated voice which, she often thought, would have been demonstrated to good advantage on the stage. She found herself believing, as always, the things he said, even when they seemed to support both sides. There was a quality of reason about Chris, and there always had been. It won him thousands of votes and several elections. It would probably win him many more when combined with his good looks. He turned to Jessica now, addressing her as he spoke of his friends, the Negro and the Mexican-American disenfranchised citizens whose power to vote he had assured by legislation whose beginnings Jess remembered. As she remembered this, she found herself briefly resenting Bick and Alvaro and others like them who attacked her husband without recalling those great acts of Chris March's in gaining permission for foreign braceros to work in California, and for illiterate children of Mexican descent to go to schools and learn to vote — "sometimes against me" he added with one of those self-deprecating and endearing laughs that won the women's vote almost wholesale.

"Now, these, my first friends," he was saying into the recorder, "sometimes ask me if I am turning my back on them because I will not see them exploited by racketeers, their meager pay — and it is far too low by today's standards — gouged from them to support greedy organizers from out-of-state. No, I say! Let them keep their pay! They need it, every cent of it. What have those rabble-rousing outsiders ever done for them that they earn the right to rob them of their small savings, the few nickels and dimes they've gotten together to get the kids a decent pair of school shoes.

The beautifully modulated sounds penetrated before their meaning did. Suddenly, as if seeing and hearing him for the first time, she thought, was he always so slick, so shoddy? Did he always appeal to the terrible, urgent needs of these people in order to keep them in their present bondage? I must have been deaf all these years. I never really heard him speak before.

He finished his talk in front of her, snapping off the mike with a waving little gesture and a smile. He was feeling so contented, so confident, he reminded her suddenly of Bethany.

Their opinions and viewpoints might be divergent, but she was her father's daughter in many ways. The resemblance, and Bethy's shocked anger at the thought, made Jessica return her husband's smile and Chris, assuming this expressed her approval, leaned over and kissed her lightly, affectionately.

"Like it, huh? Up to my old style?"

She hoped her voice did not betray the irony as she agreed, "Definitely up to your old style."

"That's my girl." He squeezed and kneaded her shoulder briefly, then fooled with the tape recorder and, as she started to get up, he reran the tape and played it back. He paced up and down the length of the room, listening to and studying his warm yet urbane voice, testing its nuances, its carefully chosen phrases, while Jess left the room unnoticed.

Dinner was formal that night and included, as an off-the-record guest, handsome Governor Simeon McClatchey, his stout, silent wife with her furtive eyes, and Dexter Dominik. "Old Sim" was nearly Chris March's age and had graduated from Cal with him. The circumstances of their mutual interest in politics of the same party had forced a close relationship between them which went under the name of "friendship."

During cocktails, Jess and D.D. did all they

could to draw the lumpish Mrs. McClatchey into the conversation and failed. Jess was therefore very proud of young Robin who attended the dinner sullenly, under protest, then managed to find in Mrs. McClatchey a surprising rooter for the university's football team.

While Jess was cutting smoothly into Bethy's attempts to needle the governor about civil rights, especially Mexican-Americans', she couldn't help feeling that the children were turning out very well indeed, in spite of the absenteeism of Chris and Jessica. Jess found herself seeing through all the political talk, finding it shallow, expedient, full of platitudes and phoney stands. She wondered if she had always felt this but failed to admit it to herself. It became necessary to step in again when the governor began to criticize Juan Alvaro and his "methods" which, as he hinted to Chris, "can put a damper on you, fellow. You've got to keep him out of these issues." And he glanced significantly at Bethany who listened with blazing eyes.

Broad-jawed Sim McClatchey was tall, brawny and while less physically handsome than Chris, had an easier way about him. People said it was impossible to be angry with Sim or to make him angry, and it had been tried by experts during the last gubernatorial campaign. He flashed his "likable, sportsman-like" grin now as D.D. kidded him about taking over as junior senator "when we move Jess up to senior senator from California. All we have to do is put the Ancient Pelican out to pasture."

The Ancient Pelican was a member of the opposition party, whom neither Chris nor D.D. nor Sim had been able to uproot in the past four terms, and Jessica, while smiling at these pipe dreams of the men present, said nothing to destroy their dreams.

Sim looked the way he had years ago when he pitched the local baseball team to a Coast championship, that is to say he looked modest but confident.

"Now there's one bright idea. Take a bit of doing though. Be easier if I just appointed myself to fill out Jess's term . . . if our girl bows out, of course."

There was a distinctly pregnant silence.

Bethy winked at her mother and giggled, an awkward sound reinforcing the fact that Sim McClatchey had thrown a verbal bomb into the center of the table. Then everyone spoke at once to cover the awkwardness.

One by one, they petered out, leaving the floor to Dexter Dominik who said, apropos of absolutely nothing, "How was the weather in the city today, Jessica? Looked clear but windy, I thought."

She wondered at his knowledge of her trip but supposed Chris or the children had told him.

D.D. went smoothly on: "Of course, one thing about San Francisco. I always duck into the hotel bars to escape the fog. They've done some regilding of those ancient panels in the Gold Room Bar. Makes the room look like a little Hall of Mirrors. Did you notice?"

Chris laughed and remarked that women like Jess and her girlfriends were usually too busy talking in the Gold Room Bar to pay attention to the gilding of a panel, but Jessica's head snapped up and as she looked across the table at D.D., her eyes narrowed. His bland, innocent face did not change, but he went on to talk about delegate strength at the coming convention.

Jessica was silenced. So D.D. knew about that scene in the Gold Room Bar this morning! How could it possibly pertain to him? Was he concerned in some way with the Alvaro affair? The fact that someone, probably the barman, had rushed to telephone D.D. as well as certain grape-growers, was more than disquieting. But was it sinister as well?

Bethy got into a low-voiced quarrel with Robin because she said he was boring everyone by his loud replay of the last Rose Bowl game, and Chris had to silence both of them. But Jessica was grateful to the children for the disturbance. It took the onus off her and she had time to think.

Coffee was served at the low empire tables in the living room and Jessica excused herself to go up and "take her medicine." Robin hurried out to the stairs to ask her if she was feeling all right. She smiled, made a fist of her hand, and pretended to swipe at his jaw.

"Don't you worry, dear. I never felt better. Keep them talking downstairs for about ten minutes if any of them want to come upstairs."

"Hey! What's your bag, Mother? You're making like 007." But he grinned and saluted. "Your orders shall be carried out, *mon general!*"

Remembering belatedly not to run up the stairs, Jess slowed down and went into her bedroom, locking the door behind her. Having also locked her dressing room door which separated her from her husband's suite, she went over to her bedside phone and started to dial the Western Press Club in San Francisco. Halfway through, she stopped, seeing herself suddenly for what she was . . .

A Judas! Funny I didn't think of that. I should have told Chris first of all, yet here I am, rushing to betray my husband's campaign manager to his enemy. The whole rotten business, if D.D. is somehow involved, could indirectly smear Chris. And he doesn't deserve that. He's worked hard to get where he is. How can I throw mud on my love, my husband, the father of my own children?

My love?

Curious that in spite of her recent terrible doubts, and the reentry of Bick Haldean into her life, she could still automatically desire to protect Chris.

After a few minutes she got up, freshened her makeup and unlocked both doors and went down to join the after-dinner group. To her amusement they were all arguing over an historic Rose Bowl game in which Cal lost to a Big Ten team on a disputed ruling. Mrs. McClatchey, Sim's albatross, was the life of the party, replaying the run and the ruling while Robin and Sim backed her up.

Jess moved over to Chris and D.D. wondering what they had their heads together about, and was relieved to find them going over Chris's upcoming speech to be delivered before the Downtown Association of San Francisco. They managed to break it up long enough to join in the good-natured wrangle over the unforgotten game, and the evening seemed likely to end as a success.

However, there were a few uneasy minutes which should have pointed the way to further trouble, as the Marches walked the McClatcheys to their modest black last-year's Cadillac.

"So long then until Tuesday," Chris said to the governor while shaking Mrs. McClatchey's hand.

"Now, let's see . . ." Sim pursed his heavy lips, and Jessica stopped speaking to Mrs. McClatchey, wondering at this departure from Sim's history of yessing her husband.

D.D. cut in. It seemed to Jessica that he was as surprised as she was.

"You will be there Tuesday, won't you, Sim? It's kind of important."

"Yeah. I know. Tough, damn it! Isn't it Monday night we're stuck to jet out East, Myrtle?"

His wife nodded. But Jessica noticed that the woman's small eyes wavered from the faces before her, avoiding them all, including her husband's.

Is that the terrorized way I've always behaved with Chris?

"That's right, Sim. Myrtie Junior graduates from the Virginia Female Academy on Wednesday —"

"Tuesday," put in the governor.

"That's right. Tuesday. It's Wednesday we are in Washington to see —" She broke off in obvious confusion.

Jessica could feel the stiffening in the two

189

bodies beside her. Both Chris and Dexter Dominik had received a blow.

"— in Washington to take in the sights — like tourists, you know," Sim explained eagerly. "Well, Myrt, let's get going. Big day tomorrow. That damned budget business. Night, folks."

They roared away into the night toward Sacramento.

Chris blew his breath out sharply, angrily. Jessica decided not to bring down his wrath on her head. Discreetly she let Dexter Dominik do that. The campaign manager was sweating in spite of the breeze off the hillside. His big teeth bit into his lower lip.

"What do you make of that?" he asked when Jessica turned away and started to the house.

She heard Chris's answer, spoken with that quiet fury which had the power to mow down those in his way: "I suppose you know who he's going to see in Washington. That cretin he's married to gave him away."

D.D. hesitated, then ventured, "The Man?"

"Who else? Christ! I thought we had The Man locked up."

"Not to mention Old Sim," Dominik murmured, looking as if he too found Chris March's white anger formidable.

"That ungrateful son of a bitch! If Sim McClatchey tries to pull the rug out from under me, I'll cut him down, so help me God! I'll destroy that bastard politically."

Greatly daring, Jessica cut in suddenly, "McClatchey seemed upset the other day by the trouble with the farm laborers. He may be swayed now by the attack on Alvaro."

Chris turned swiftly, his blue eyes bright with fury.

"Jess, keep out of this. This is no business for women. Dex and I have got to do a little fence-mending. We have work . . ."

Jessica, amazed at her own nerve and feeling her face redden with the violence of her response, laughed and startled him. The sound of her laughter was mocking, brittle, hideous in such a moment. "Don't talk like that to your senator, my boy!"

She swung around and walked rapidly toward the house where their loud voices had brought Bethy and Robin to the living room windows and her own nurse trotting out, waving a small bottle, apparently glycerine or some other gruesome antidote.

"Mom!" Bethy cried in a strangled voice. "Are you all right? Don't get excited, Mommie."

Jess waved at the children, trying in vain, to keep them from their panicky gallop to the door to meet her.

"I'm fine, fine. Your father's had a little

trouble, that's all . . . political trouble."

Nevertheless, she was shaking all over and along with the other matters that troubled her, she was frankly dreading the next confrontation with Chris. Never in their married life had she defied him in this way, or added to his already troubled consciousness. Usually, when she had tried to defy him, she wished a second later to withdraw the challenge. Tonight, somewhat to her own shocked amazement, she withdrew nothing, though she hated the necessity for the quarrel and even more, for hurting him, as she knew she had.

Behind her Chris and D.D. talked in low tones. Their voices seemed to fade away. She hoped her husband's temper had likewise faded to a cool, reasonable degree. No matter how much in the right she might consider herself, she had no wish to go through another few minutes like the last ones.

In the house she waved the children away and would have waved away the nurse's stern hatchet-face but was followed up the stairs by the woman. She took what the nurse gave her, let water — tepid and revolting — be run for her, and swallowed the capsule. The nurse glanced behind into the faintly lighted staircase, obviously looking for her hero, ex-senator Christopher March.

"Please go along, thank you," Jessica said

calmly, smiling until the woman had gone out of her sight. Then she went in and this time did not bother to lock the door. She knew she would not see Chris that night.

She went across the room, opened the drapes and studied the distant lights of Oakland, then, blurred by the night fog, the Bay Bridge lights and the island of Yerba Buena, she saw the hilly skyline of San Francisco.

Bick? Are you over there somewhere in the canyons of the City? Shall I ruin my husband's whole career to support your Juan Alvaro, a man I hardly know?

She did not ask herself if Bick thought of her at all. That way led to adultery . . .

She turned away from the windows, drew the drapes shut and was about to cross the room when, for no reason that she could recall, she suddenly thought of that fantastic tale Augusta March had told Bethany: "You are like your mother. You will have to buy a husband."

On an impulse Jess went over to the telephone while she still had the courage, and looked up her mother-in-law's area code. In a minute or two she had Augusta March's Maryland number and started to dial.

– ELEVEN –

The telephone rang so long it gave Jessica a chance to cool off, but unhappily, she only used the minutes to grow hotter with resentment. When Augusta March's voice came on, with its suggestion of Maryland softness overlaying the bell tones of her California heritage, Jessica was so worked up she wondered why her mother-in-law sounded sleepy.

"Y-es? Good heavens! Is this you, Jessica?" The voice sharpened with embarrassing solicitude. "Are you all right, dear?"

"I'm all right. We're all fine. I mean — physically."

"My God, girl! Do you know what time it is? Ten after two. I know you young people are night owls, but —"

Jessica hadn't been included in the description "young people" for some time and upon any other occasion would have delighted in it, but now she blurted out before she could lose the impetus and courage of her anger, "Augusta, I've been terribly upset by something Bethany told me."

The older woman was clearly all at sea. She yawned. "Look, dear, couldn't this wait until morning? Or is it —" excitement edged her voice again, "is it something about Chris's campaign?"

That *would* get to her, Jess told herself but she knew perfectly well this had always been a prime factor in her own happiness or her anxiety.

"No, it's something else." She caught her breath and rushed on. "Bethany told me something you said to her in Baltimore last year . . . about buying husbands."

"Look, dear — excuse me while I find my cigarettes. I'm simply famished for a smoke. . . . There!" Jessica heard little sounds over the phone and then her mother-in-law's voice again. "Ah! That's better. Now then. My grandchild wants to buy a husband? With her looks?"

Jess pursued the matter doggedly. "At her age I'm told I had looks. But apparently someone bought me a husband."

There was a little stillness and then: "Jessica! What a way to put it! If you had any notion of history, you'd know these things are called dowries. Dowries, dear! Are you still with me?"

"All the way," Jessica answered, adding privately, and way past "go." What was this dowry business? "I don't know if you remember me when I was engaged to Chris, but the last thing in the world I had was money, a dowry as you call it."

"Of course not. And I do remember those days. But Thea Souza and I wanted our children to have a good start. It would have taken Chris years longer to make his start if it hadn't been for your mother's — what else can I call it? Your dowry. Now, dear, go to bed and forget it."

There was an unmistakeable click, and Jessica found herself thinking, I don't blame you. Poor Augusta, being aroused at two A.M. to be hounded by questions on something that happened eighteen years ago!

Voices startled her in the hall, and she was sure she heard Chris and then Robin's anxiety-pitched voice, "No. Let me do it. Let me, Father."

A knock followed and Robin called, "Are you all right, Mother?"

"Yes. I'm fine. Tell everyone good night, dear."

Drained of all feeling except cynicism, she asked herself, is it possible after I snapped at him in his most vulnerable place that Chris cares how I am? I bought him — or, more correctly, Mother seems to have bought him for me, yet he can pretend he cares now? What an actor!"

She bathed, went to bed, lay there wondering a long while where Thea Souza had got the "dowry" which bought Chris. The information from Augusta explained so much that had always puzzled Jess. Why *had* Christopher March, college graduate, son of a politically oriented mother, chosen to marry that little, half-educated nobody who was a cashier in the theater her mother managed for the Fox West Coast chain?

Considering those long years of their marriage, Jess could not deny that Chris had seemed happy. And she had to admit, in the darkness of her bed that much of her present dissatisfaction was rooted in her mature realization of desires unfulfilled. At her present age of thirty-five and faced with the knowledge that another attractive man was sexually drawn to her, Jessica felt all the errors and failure of her marriage more clearly than before. More clearly perhaps than they actually existed. She was analytical enough to realize that.

But the blow about the dowry was a serious one.

"Honestly now, face it!" she told herself. "Has your own husband, the father of Robin and Bethy, ever really loved you? Or was it always his sense of a debt? The paying back of what Thea Gribble Souza bought when she purchased Christopher March for her daughter?"

Chris was a man of honor; he would feel obligated. That made it doubly painful: to love a man for eighteen years and then find he had never, even early in their marriage, loved her! It had all been the fulfillment of an obligation.

It was a long night, one she would never forget. But for some curious reason, she felt stronger afterward. Perhaps, she told herself, because all the doubts and wonderings of half her lifetime were now erased. There could be no doubt remaining.

Bick Haldean called Jessica the next day while she was at breakfast with Bethy and a quiet, but exceedingly polite Chris who had not mentioned their mutual recriminations of the night before. Dexter Dominik had stayed the night in a guest room and having breakfasted in bed, was busy, according to Chris, making calls to important lobbyists in Washington.

Robin had already eaten and rushed off to Berkeley to a sidewalk bazaar for the benefit of the Student Victims of Police Brutality. The brutality in this case had been a trifle vague but the unrest was concrete, and Robin was to handle the counter which sold handmade paper mini-dresses to coeds.

When Jessica's telephone rang upstairs, the

sound was confused and muffled by closed doors and the long staircase. Both Chris and Bethy supposed the call was for them. Bethy started, her eyes bright, and asked to be excused. She murmured to her mother, "I'm sure it's Bick, for me. I've been at him to take me over to interview Mr. and Mrs. Alvaro. They're staying in town until it's safe to move back, you know."

In her enthusiasm Bethy slid her chair back and spoke loudly enough to be audible to Chris who had asked the new maid to answer the phone.

Chris said now in his quiet way, "Bethany, I don't want you to be seeing those people until we know more about what really happened in that explosion."

"What happened!" Bethy repeated, her young voice cracking in falsetto with her passion. "Some stinking scab tried to blow them up. That's what happened!"

"Not necessarily. I'm told it's altogether likely that Alvaro deliberately returned to the house for his briefcase. That, in fact, Alvaro himself had been quarreling with the business agent over use of the funds solicited from the public. If so, I needn't tell you what a monstrous deception your hero is —"

"It's a call for Senator March," the maid explained from the doorway.

199

The interruption was a lucky one. Bethy had just begun a denunciation of her father's "fiendish" theory and was issuing blanket denials of everything, but Jess said, "Bethy, be quiet. Wiser heads than yours are looking into all the angles," and the girl seemed to catch some hidden meaning, as though she and her mother had secrets from her father. She gave her father a quick glance as he got up from the table, but the maid coughed and cleared up her ambiguous statement.

"Excuse me. The call is for Mrs. Senator March."

"Oh, of course," Chris said with tawny eyebrows raised, and sat down again while Bethy grinned triumphantly.

Jessica went up the stairs very conscious that, for the first time in several years, Chris had watched her go and appeared extremely uneasy over her secrecy. She told herself his uneasiness stemmed from political doubts, perhaps even his dangerous conversation with Bethany, but still, there was this evidence of his interest, and she was delighted with that, no matter what his motives were.

Still she had an enormous sense of guilt when she answered the phone in her bedroom with the hall door open and heard Bick Haldean's very masculine voice speaking to her with its warm suggestion of virility.

"How are you feeling, Jess?"

Surprised she said, "Fine!" Her problems at present, were entirely mental, or at worst emotional. She still hadn't put together the whole story of the dowry, and this, with corresponding matters that threatened her marriage, made the consideration of her physical ailments almost laughable.

"Why?" she asked, suddenly aware of his tension. "Is something wrong?"

"Not yet. Not publicly. It's about our friend whose wife we met. Remember?"

"Of course I remember!" He must think she was losing her mind. "At the airport. You mean —" She broke off, aware belatedly that it was conceivable someone could listen in on the extension in her combined sewing room and office down the hall. The room was not far from D.D.'s guest room, and it was exactly the sort of thing Dexter Dominik was capable of, and he had been given plenty of time to go from this guest room to her office to listen in.

"Is she all right? Has anything happened?"

"Not yet, but she is worried about — ah — gossip after her — accident. Can I meet you somewhere and take you to see her and her family?"

Feeling like a spy and a traitor in her own home, Jessica looked hurriedly over her shoulder. The stairs creaked, but they always had. She wished she had closed the door.

"Shall I pick you up somewhere nearby?" he asked.

The line buzzed oddly and Bick's voice sounded far off. The line had sounded this way before when Robin or Bethy accidentally picked up the handy extension in Jessica's office to make a call.

"No!" She knew he guessed what had happened, that they must be discreet. "Remember the place where you met Bethy yesterday?"

He was momentarily confused, then said abruptly, "When she called to me . . ." He hesitated. "Okay. How soon?"

She thought she could make it early in the afternoon, allowing for the time it would take to throw off D.D. who, if he was listening in, would undoubtedly follow her. Setting the phone back she thought of Robin and his usual remarks about 007 and James Bond. Robin was nearer right than he thought. . . .

Jessica did not make the mistake of rushing madly off to San Francisco, but explained to everyone that the Party was getting up a committee of women voters to try and influence the upcoming convention on the matter of a civil rights stand that would satisfy the moderates and the liberals. Dexter Dominik, who came in to check with Chris on a new address for a Sacramento lobby, grinned toothily at Jessica's statement.

"If you can satisfy both sides, senator, you ought to be active on the farm labor problem. I'm sure the Croisetti people and the Duvauxs and even Señor Alvaro would welcome you."

Bethy put in, talking to herself, "I can't figure what's happened to Bick. I told him I wanted to go see the pickets and maybe help out."

"God forbid!" Chris murmured but said nothing to Jess until she was leaving. He made it a point to linger around the old-fashioned back rumpus room which she had to pass in going down the back stairs to the garage. She was more than surprised, almost shaken, when, after they kissed in the perfunctory way of an old married couple, Chris's blue eyes studied her face oddly, intently. It was strange because she often suspected he didn't even see her when he looked her way.

"All this running around isn't exactly what the doctor ordered, is it?"

She could not resist the cool counter-question, "Why? Does it matter? Can I be of more use to you and the party at home?"

His features stiffened to their usual reserve,

and he turned away. "Certainly not. But when you agreed to play this part, this senator business, it was never meant to be the real thing. All this coming and going, meetings, speeches, committees . . . it's rough on —"

"Don't worry," she promised him lightly as she rustled down the stairs. "I won't interfere with your precious plans."

"That's not what I meant," he called after her, his anger clearly audible to her as she reached the garage door.

She wondered as she drove away if he knew the whole story of the "dowry." But, of course, he must know it. Why else would Chris — the idol of every female in sight of him — marry Jessica Souza? He had to know about the dowry. Everything would have been impossible if he hadn't known. As she drove down into town and toward the freeway she tried to think back to the still-painful days of her mother's death and funeral. That was eleven years ago and Jess hadn't expected an inheritance of any kind except Thea's love, her passionate desire for her daughter "to be happy, and to live," she told Jessica and Chris "a whole lot better than Jess's father and I did. He was a good man, and he meant well. But money's so goddamned important. You kids okay now?"

The "kids," standing by her bedside in the

hospital, assured her that they were fine. Chris as a congressman from California, headed for the next step, junior senator from the state.

"You know something? You'll be president of the old U.S.A. yet," Thea had assured Chris, with that wonderful smile she always had, even on her deathbed. Jessica closed her eyes hard for an instant.

Mother . . . I know you did it for me . . . I know.

She wondered suddenly if she wished her mother hadn't provided that dowry. And where did Mother get it? What would the life of Jessica Souza have been like if Chris hadn't wanted her? How strange to think of Robin and Bethany with another father!

It can't be true! It can't be!

But, of course, it was. She had known it the minute she began to talk to Augusta March. She turned her attention to the rapidly crowding streets ahead as they converged on the freeway to the bridge ramps. Curious . . . there was a deep blue Volkswagen following behind her that looked exactly like Robin's, with the blue and gold streamers from last fall's big game still trailing off the outside rear-view mirror. There were many blue Volkswagens at the University of California whose chauvinists made other colors like red especially unpopular, since red was the color of their ancient rival, Stanford. It couldn't be Robin. He had left early for the campus in a friend's aged M.G. But could it be someone else, using Robin's car?

She could not make out the driver; another car, a Mustang, cut rather nastily between them, and when she did not see the little blue car again she assumed she had been mistaken. Still, it was just the sort of thing one might suspect Dexter Dominik of doing: a sneaking, underhanded, spying trick. She wondered if he had told Chris about her meeting yesterday with Bick and Pete Tognazzi — not that Chris would have been jealous. She wished very much that he might have been! That will be the day! she told herself grimly.

Once on the long, many-laned approach to the toll plaza of the bridge, she was able to make out the cars behind her. She was surprised suddenly to see the same blue Volkswagen, now at a slight distance behind her as if making it a point not to pass her. She slowed down to pay the toll and stalling for time, adjusted the rear-view mirror with unsteady fingers.

"Sorry, lady," said the young toll-taker, easing his complaint with a smile. "Afraid you'll have to move on."

He was right. Three cars were forming a nervous train behind her. She pulled away and dashed up toward the Yerba Buena tunnel. She knew she couldn't lose the blue Volkswagen on the bridge, but once she turned off the nearest ramp, she could lose herself in the warren of little before-the-fire streets around the Embarcadero. She turned sharply at the First Street ramp and smiled with satisfaction to see that the blue Volkswagen had not made the turn in time and was jogging on.

How is that for outwitting the great D.D.? she silently taunted the faraway little blue bug.

– TWELVE –

She drove around the Embarcadero, past the
Ferry Building, and doubled back to come into
the garage from above Union Square. Bick and
Peter Tognazzi were waiting for her at the
garage ramp. Bick took her hands, looked
her up and down and then shook her hands
tightly.

"You look lovely, Jess. Are you feeling
better?"

"Invigorated!" she said with a bite to the
word.

He studied her and she guessed she had
worried him by her new attitude. But why
not? She felt herself to be a new woman,
hardened, able to endure. She had already
endured the worst discovery of her marriage. She thought it strange now that she
couldn't react more enthusiastically to
Bick's concern for her. He was everything
that Chris was not, and his reactions were
those she had long dreamed of from Chris;
yet all she felt at this minute was a passionate desire to get on with the business
at hand.

"If I'm a senator," she said more or less

to herself, "It's time I was doing some investigating on my own — to earn my salary." Unorthodox, and a little late, but still she was sincere about it. "Where are the Alvaros?" she asked abruptly, looking from Bick to an anxious, tense Pete Tognazzi. "Have you found out anything? Because if you haven't, I've got a little bombshell to toss in."

Bick looked behind her. She thought it was an extraordinarily furtive gesture, and she decided to prick all this masculine pretense: "I think it's Dexter Dominik who is following me. He knows all about our little doings yesterday in the Gold Room Bar."

They were walking toward what proved to be Pete Tognazzi's car, a three-year-old Chevy, snuggled up to Bick's own white T-bird classic. Pete said plaintively, "That joker prowling the beat again?"

She explained that D.D. had known all about their meeting, and doubtless their entire conversation. "I think it was the barman. Everything D.D. knows could have come from him. It's logical. No one else could have known what D.D. knows."

"She knows a lot more than we do," Bick told Pete, silencing him as the investigator started to question her.

"We'll take my jalopy," Pete said opening the rear door. Jess climbed in automatically, rather resenting the businesslike treatment she was receiving. She felt that she had given them some important information in her disclosure of D.D.'s spying activities, but all they wanted to do was get on with their original plans.

Bick looked back at her from the front seat beside Pete. "All okay?"

"Certainly." She hoped she did not sound as stiff and resentful as she felt. The recent discoveries about her marriage had depressed her so much she was beginning to doubt everyone.

"Don't forget. Keep back, darling — or is it still Jess?"

She grinned at him for his mistake, but ducked back to keep hidden. She had not liked being stuck away alone in this back seat, but now understood the necessity for keeping her presence with them a secret. They drove out Geary toward Sutro Heights where Jess caught an invigorating, if chilling breath of the ocean beyond and wished she had worn something warmer than her silk sheath. She shivered when Pete Tognazzi stopped abruptly on a side street off Geary, and they all piled out in front of a clean stucco house with red trim that was built over its garage in the San Francisco way.

They went up the long flight of steps, Bick taking Jessica's arm in a proprietary way. Jess grinned mischievously, and Bick, though smiling back at her, asked what struck her so funny.

"The way you take my arm in that very correct way. So like Chris."

That shook him. He drew away from her momentarily, then put his arm around her waist and pulled tight. She yelped but was not displeased. She wanted to say, "That's better!" but didn't. She had been feeling so low that Bick's unequivocal interest in her was both welcome and warming.

The door opened so quickly Jess knew someone had been watching for their arrival. Juan Alvaro himself met them, shaking hands all around and ushering them into an old-fashioned front room whose big, square window gave a fabulous view of the ocean breakers north of Seal Rocks and the fog banks piled on the horizon.

"This is Manny's brother's house. They have been very good to us," said the beautiful Mrs. Alvaro, coming to the window behind Jess. In spite of Jessica's knowledge of the injury from flying glass, it was a shock to see the white bandage, two inches square, that marred Mrs. Alvaro's face.

"Manny?" Jess repeated, finding the nickname vaguely familiar in an uncomfortable way.

"Manuel Caporetta died in the car when the bomb exploded."

Jessica reddened in embarrassment, wondering when her mind would achieve some kind of order and especially prompt her memory. She apologized and then, driven by guilt at her own indifference to the unfortunate major victim of the bombing, she prompted Mrs. Alvaro: "I imagine Bick told you that I overheard something about the plot."

Mrs. Alvaro gently moved her back behind the neat, starched window curtains, speaking as she did so. "Yes. We were very grateful. Excuse me, but someone may be set to watch the house any time, and we want to be sure none of us are seen at the windows. Luckily, we have a good view here of anyone who might try to, as my husband calls it, put a tail on us."

Jess was surprised that the dead business agent's family was protecting the Alvaros, and she tried to say so without suggesting that there might have been bitterness or suspicion against Juan Alvaro. Alvaro himself heard Jessica's remark as he talked with Bick and Pete Tognazzi. He said in a kind of bleak and quiet triumph, "That at least proves these latest charges to be lies. Manny's family know who is really to blame."

Mrs. Alvaro's dark eyes flashed. "Can you

imagine the lengths they will go to? Saying Juan himself rigged the explosive charge to kill Manny? Of course, they quarreled occasionally, but they had been friends ever since Galileo High. But Juan's enemies will do anything, anything to ruin us. They tell the most fantastic lies."

A woman who had, heretofore, remained in the shadow of an inner hall, moved toward Jess and Mrs. Alvaro now and gently touched the bandage on Mrs. Alvaro's head. The white gauze was a bright contrast to the smooth olive skin of the woman's cheek.

"I am Mrs. Caporetta," the quiet, middle-aged woman introduced herself. She was short and a bit stout, with that comfortable look which made one like her instantly. She was in black, but her attention was all for the Alvaros. "If it were not for you, Senator March," she said warmly, "we would still be fighting in the dark, not knowing where to look. We would not even have men like Pete here to help us."

Pete put in succinctly, "Got to have evidence. Got to start somewhere. The senator started us. That's it. Bick, Juan, do we begin?"

Juan Alvaro cleared off the round maple table in the center of the dining room which was separated from the front room by old-fashioned wooden buttresses and said, "Put the recorder here." And to his wife, "*Querida*, we should ask the senator to sit here, near the sound box, don't you think?"

Jessica let herself be maneuvered to the table and the others stood around her. She still did not know what she was expected to do and wondered suspiciously if they were somehow going to use her own recording of the conversation with Bick and Pete yesterday.

Pete explained rapidly as they all watched him examine a cassette and place it in the little recorder.

"Mrs. Alvaro went to a restaurant in Sonoma yesterday with Gladys Duvaux and a bunch of other wives in the wine business. The dames did a lot of talking, sympathizing with Mrs. Alvaro and all that. It was one of those things where the women soft-soap while the men are out cutting throats. Anyway, she recorded their voices. You may find they sound different on a recording, but if you could pick out that Puddles dame —"

Nervous but careful not to show it, Jessica nodded, and then stared at the recorder, trying to envision the women through the muffled and unfamiliar sound of the recorded voices. The knowedge that everyone in the room appeared to be hanging breathless on her identification gave her a chill. She felt them all studying her every reaction, waiting, listening, judging her every time she took a breath.

The recording was a gaggle of indistinct female voices, each cutting into the other until she got Mrs. Alvaro's clear tones and then Gladys Duvaux who twittered, "We're blood sisters now, no matter what our husbands row about. I've got my bandages and you've got yours." And then, louder, Gladys's voice called, "Girls, it was ghastly. Simply ghastly! Elena will tell you what we went through."

Jess heard Mrs. Caporetta's hard breathing behind her, as the widow relived the callous description of her husband's death, but when Jess looked around anxiously, the widow smiled, shook her head, and Jess returned her attention to the recorder.

Some unidentified voice had asked hopefully, "Tell! Tell!"

Elena Alvaro's voice very cleverly asked, "Do you really want to hear? It's such a terrible thing."

And then, as Gladys Duvaux asked each of several women, their gushing replies punctuated by shivers came clearly out of the recorder.

"Play those again," Jessica ordered Pete who snapped buttons, rewound and played back the last sixty seconds or so.

"Can you tell which one is Puddles?" he asked her.

She was too much aware of the tension in those around the table, but she moistened her lips and said positively, "None of them." She was sure they would all leap onto her verbally with assurances that she had goofed up somewhere and missed the voice.

But no one said anything except Pete who demanded roughly, "You sure? You absolutely sure?"

"Of course, I'm sure!" she said crossly because she was so worried. She hated to be placed in this sort of position where her simple identification meant too much to so many people. Chris was the hero of the family, the public idol. He should be doing this kind of thing.

To her amazement, the short, sharp answer she gave them relieved everybody. Bick patted her on the back, and the two Alvaros shook her hand. Pete looked positively cheerful, unlike his dark and gloomy self.

"Of course she's sure!" he repeated to them all. "So we've got it pinned down to that one dame named Puddles. She's due back in town tonight from Rome. I'm told Clormann wired her to stay away, but she was in flight; they couldn't reach her. They're sure to hide her out somewhere. Especially if they got our conversation yesterday in the bar."

"If Dexter Dominik did, I'm sure Puddles's gang must know by now," Jessica put in.

"Does that mean you know it was this Puddles's husband who is back of it all?"

"Probably — and that means Clormann and the eastern syndicate, not our local people," Juan Alvaro murmured to his wife with great relief. "Do you realize, if it turns out that only the Croisetti owners are involved, we needn't go on mistrusting the people we've known all our lives? I'd give almost anything if we could prove the Duvauxs and the Deltas and the other Californians aren't involved."

"These patriots!" Pete said with his dry laugh. "You don't care if you get blown up, just as long as it's not by a friend."

Mrs. Alvaro glanced lovingly at her husband. "That about sums up Juanito's view of the world."

Pete had been fumbling with an old ten-inch record on the stereo set in one wall of the front room. It played at 78-speed and the tone was scratchy but almost immediately, amid laughter and the jingle of ice cubes, came a breathy voice that was a hideous parody of the late Marilyn Monroe.

"That's it!" Jess cried. "That's the voice I heard behind me, talking about an execution, a killing."

The Alvaros smiled. Mrs. Alvaro said, "You needn't play any more, Pete. It was just one of those silly joke records we made at a Christmas party last year. We cut this record and then nobody liked his — and especially her — voice. It was the woman called Puddles that you just identified. She does have a distinctive, breathy style, like that blonde movie star."

To Jessica, it seemed a small thing she had been able to accomplish on this run across town, but they were inordinately happy about it and she was touched to discover that their happiness stemmed from their genuine concern over the innocence of their lifelong acquaintances. Yet, so far as Jess had observed, the Duvauxs and others were ready enough to accept the necessity for Juan Alvaro's death.

The Alvaros offered cocktails, but to Jessica's surprise, Bick refused for both of them.

"The senator and I have a few political problems to iron out. I'm one of her constituents, you know."

Pete said, "Leave my jalopy in the garage. I'm going to go over this mess with Juan. I'll get a cab into town."

Jess caught just the faintest exchange of glances between the Alvaros, although they were obviously ashamed of their own suspicions, but Jess was far from resenting them. Her own emotions were so mixed, so twisted, and thoughts of her marriage so painful, she was almost relieved that the Alvaros' suspicions and her own coincided.

Let it be taken out of my hands, she thought with uneasy excitement. If Bick wants me, he, at least, wants me more than I was ever wanted by Chris! She wondered how far she would go, whether she would actually betray Chris, her vows, her children, if she were strongly tempted. Was Bick that temptation?

Juan Alvaro's quiet voice broke into her tormented and dangerous thoughts. "You have never asked me, senator, if I was responsible for the bombing at my bungalow."

Confused she stammered, "I never th-thought of it. And besides, Mrs. Caporetta —" Jess looked at the widow who smiled faintly. "I never b-believed you had anything to do with it, Mr. Alvaro."

"Possibly you didn't, but I wanted you to know, anyway." He looked across the room at his wife who was putting away the Christmas party record and talking to Pete about it. Jessica liked his expression of tenderness and pride as he studied Elena Alvaro. He caught Jessica's sympathetic gaze and added, "She is the one who kept me at it when the going was bad. She is still the one who refused to quit. When I felt the explosion the other day and came rushing out, I saw blood streaming down her face. She was swaying, but when I took her in my arms she cried, 'Fight them! Fight them!' When the farm laborers of this state are recognized, it will be my wife who did it, by prodding us. She and I will be down in the San Joaquin tomorrow night at the mass meeting. Without my Elena," he motioned to Mrs. Caporetta with his other outstretched hand, "and my dear Maria, there would be nothing. We would be back where we were in the early fifties."

Chris March had often said much the same thing about Jessica, but never, she thought, with this deep, passionate sincerity. Jess was rudely shaken out of her admiration for the hard-working Alvaros by Pete Tognazzi who went out to see, as he put it, "if it was safe for Bick and Jessica to leave." It was so like a scene from a gangster epic, with Pete looking furtively around the house, the steps, and finally the street, that all of it made Jess a little sick. She said so when she and Bick finally got into Pete's car, and she watched Pete duck back up the steps and into the house.

"It's hideous! I never dreamed things like this could happen under our very noses. We might as well be in some gangster movie."

"Honey, we are in a gangster movie! There was something extremely gangsterish about Manny Caporetta's death, don't you think?"

"Happy thought!" she muttered wryly and slid down a little in her seat. "I do believe I'm an incurable coward."

He looked at her. She could not mistake the look. His free hand moved to hers as she busied herself fastening her safety belt. "Don't you go insulting the female I love." His hand held hers so tightly, her wedding band and engagement ring cut into her finger, and as she winced he said brusquely, "Sorry," and let her go. On impulse, she put her left hand up and closed her fingers on his arm; she felt his muscles stiffen under her touch.

"Don't be sorry. I'm not." He looked straight ahead but she knew she was not wrong about the strength of his reaction. She laughed softly. "It was the sight of my rings that made me wince like that."

"What?"

"It occurred to me suddenly that I probably bought my own engagement ring."

"Jess!"

"Well, it's truer than you think." She sighed and stared out at the passing cars. "I don't believe Chris ever loved me, even at first. I'm being frank, you see."

"Look, Jess . . . darling?" He glanced at her but Geary Street was getting congested and he had to lean on the horn and turn his attention to the traffic ahead.

Jessica began to laugh as Bick swore at a Jaguar that cut in ahead of them, and pretty soon he laughed too. He said, "Never mind. My day will come."

She felt wanted and warm and daring.

"You bet!" It was a silly reply, the kind of slang she used in her girlhood, and it clearly reminded Bick of those days.

The ride in was far pleasanter than the outward trip.

They were stopped by a traffic jam on Van Ness and had to wait for the wide avenue to be cleared of a Kharmann-Ghia and a Porsche which had come together on the theory of the irresistible versus the immovable.

"Dumb kids!" Bick muttered, but he was on the verge of a smile.

Jessica laughed. "That's exactly the sort of thing my two 'dumb kids' might do." She considered him and went on thoughtfully, "I wonder what kind of a father you'd have made. You may discover you're a born bachelor."

He startled her by his rude and snappish answer, "Speak for the Sainted Christopher. You've never given yourself a chance to know whether I'd made a good father or not. I'd have given anything on God's earth to have a sunny-haired, passionate, loving child like little Bethy."

That shook her out of her playful mood. Bethany would be sure her mother had played the serpent, stolen Bethy's "boyfriend." It was a hideous tangle. She was relieved when the wrecks, the arguments and the participants had been removed and the police waved Bick on. He and Jess had little to say as they rode toward Union Square, yet the feeling between them was tense and full of awareness, each aware of the other in a dangerously sensual way.

"There," Bick indicated with his head. "That's where I hole up, the Western Press Club."

She looked out at the old, brick, six-story building and wondered which windows belonged to Bick. She asked him.

"Fourth floor. The two windows on the left there. Not bad for a bachelor."

She laughed. "Sounds pretty small. What do you do for visitors?"

He did not glance at her. "How about looking it over, giving it your okay? I've a feeling it needs a woman's touch."

"Marvelous," she said lightly. "I'd love to. Senator March in a men's club? I'd really be on everybody's tongue."

"Well?"

"That means no, darling. You know I wouldn't dare."

"Don't call me darling!" he said with sudden, surprising anger. "Unless you mean it."

She put her hand over his where it rested on the wheel. She had a dreadful impulse to cry, and when she spoke she couldn't control the twist of emotion in her voice. "Bick? Sometimes I go back. I mean . . . in my m-mind. I wonder if I made an awful m-mistake the night we fought."

"You mean the night you fought me off!" After a few seconds he added, "I'm a patient guy. It's not too late."

He loved me. He loved me then and he loves me today — and I failed him because I had an idiotic passion for a man who had to be bribed to marry me!

They drove into the underground garage at Union Square and Bick parked the car, according to the arrangement, as near as possible to its previous stall. He helped Jessica out and they walked, arm in arm, toward her own car in a distant stall on the same level.

"Don't go back," he said, his voice sounding sharp and urgent in the hollow area of the parking level.

"I've got to. There's my family. They . . . need me."

"Do they? Bethany and Robin are nearly grown . . . and you won't pretend *he* needs you."

"Don't!" The words and the truth she suspected in them were like knife cuts.

They had almost reached her car when he pulled her to him. She made a token resistance, mostly because the rough authoritative gesture surprised her by its timing. There might be witnesses coming down the ramp at any minute. When he took her head and framed it between his rough hands, her lips trembled. But when his own mouth crushed hers hard, as if to make a violent entry, she felt herself responding with all the passion of her lost years.

It must have been a mere matter of seconds but it seemed to encompass a lifetime of dreams and hopes in this strange, momentary fulfillment before they drew apart, startled by the sound of a shoe grating upon the stone floor behind them. With the nervous feminine gesture of a hand to her dishevelled hair, Jessica looked around. She heard Bick's quick intake of breath at the same time that she saw the little blue Volkswagen — and standing in front of it, both Bethany and Chris.

– THIRTEEN –

All Jessica's excuses, the failure she saw in her marriage, her uneasy thoughts in which she could not deny the temptation of Bick's love, now seemed far away. It was as if she had been actually taken in adultery. She felt deathly ill, with a shame greater even than she had known during the early days of her marriage when her gauche youth had embarrassed her ambitious husband.

She moved away from Bick, wondering why he made it so difficult for her, holding her to the last. He looked oddly like Chris at this soundless numbing minute in time, his facial muscles stiff, terrible in their frozen emotion-dried way. It was this realization, and perhaps the angry glitter in Bethany's very adult eyes that shook Jessica out of her self-accusing terror. She managed to speak to Bick as calmly as if nothing lay between them, not even the dangerous revival of an old infatuation.

"Good-bye for now, Bick. I'll give you a call about the investigation." She had started off toward her own car, though she would have to pass her husband and daughter to reach it. She turned briefly, astonished at her own sharp decisiveness. "I'll talk to you about the investigation and everything else."

"Jess?" Bick called but she paid no more attention to him. She was almost glad this crisis had been reached. She was determined to have it out with Chris at once, in spite of the almost psychopathic dread she had always felt at the idea of Chris turning his freezing anger and contempt upon her. It had seldom happened in their lives together, but when it did occur she never forgot it. It was this dread which had forced her to bottle up all the feelings, the bitterness and resentments that should have been brought out long ago.

She let her pent-up resentments carry her to face Chris who was looking unusually white as they confronted each other. He moistened his lips nervously. This sign of his inner turbulence gave her both satisfaction and the old twist of pain she had always felt at any indication of her husband's suffering.

Her voice surprised her by its calm: "I'm going to drive home, Chris. I suppose you'll be taking Robin's car."

"Jess, we've got to —" Chris stopped. She had never seen him so incoherent. For one breathtaking instant she prayed that his incoherence was due to his genuine affection for her, even the thought of losing her. The hope was so real she felt dizzy with the painful joy of it.

Everyone made a jerking grab at her, and she wondered if she had swayed, given some indication of illness. She hated her body for betraying an inner confusion. Psychosomatic, she assured herself . . . it's all in my mind.

But the shock of seeing her like this had certainly shaken Chris. The frozen anger was gone, leaving concern, anxiety.

"I'm going home," she repeated too loudly. "We can settle things then." She felt her face break into a faint smile for Bethy. When the girl only gulped, staring at her, Jess shrugged and walked firmly to her car. She heard Bick stalking across the floor behind her but ignored him.

Bethy and Chris whispered together. Jess glanced at her family as Bick reached behind her and opened her car door. She was just in time to see Chris nudge Bethy, insisting on something. Jess thanked Bick briskly with a monosyllable and got in. As she turned the key, Bethany came fluttering up in front of the car waving her arms, her gold charm bracelets flashing across the air. Jess remained still, hoping against hope that Bethy wanted to go with her.

Bick and Bethany confronted each other

briefly, then Bick walked around the car and opened the door opposite Jess. Bethy climbed in beside her mother. "Let me come too, Mom?"

"Why not?"

Meanwhile, Jessica saw Chris getting into the little blue Volkswagen. Was it possible he had asked Bethy to ride with her mother? He was behaving oddly for Christopher March, emotional, queerly unlike his cold, imperturbable self. But of course! She realized with belated cynicism that he was afraid of a scandal and divorce. It would react first against Senator Jessica March, then, destroying her use to him as the moving spirit of the convention. Then, a scandal which besmirched her would ultimately lose him President Walters's all-important endorsement.

"Are you feeling all right, Mom?" Bethany asked, upset by Jessica's long silence as they made their way home amid the late-afternoon traffic.

Jessica said, "I'm f-fine. I wish you and your father would stop assuming my h-health must be impaired in order for a male to kiss me."

In a hollow little voice, Bethy murmured plaintively, "Is that all it was? Just a kiss?" I figured it must be. Bick wouldn't —"

"No. That isn't all it was. Or at least, all it might have been."

Bethy gave her a quick, puzzled look. "Don't pretend with me, Mom, please. All this hard, cold bit — it isn't you, not really. And I'm beginning to see why you made Bick kiss you. It was to bug Father, wasn't it?"

"I made Bick kiss me!" Jess felt that she had never been so humiliated, or so angry in her life. Surely this was the depths in degradation, to have everyone believe her so inadequate as a woman that she had to force men to kiss her for some unnamed purpose.

"Yes, Mom. You saw Father and me and you wanted to make Father angry or jealous — I don't blame you a bit — and you kissed Bick. Father told me why you kissed Bick. Only . . ." she considered thoughtfully, "what were you doing with Bick during the time we missed you? Father said you were undercutting him with the grape-growers. Is that what it was?"

Jessica sighed and gave up the pretense of the tough adultress. "We were with the Alvaros. I had some evidence to give them. It may not be much, but it put them on the right track. Or so they said."

Bethy moved closer to her, enthusiasm bubbling again. "That's it! Father was right, in a way. I should have known. Oh, Mom! You shouldn't pretend with me. You're wonderful!"

"Sure. I shouldn't pretend." She was tired of her little act of indifference as well. The numbness and indignation and coldness had worn off. She had never felt more tired, or more sick at the ashes that remained of her married life.

When they reached home Chris was already there. He still looked peaked and he seemed older than usual in the gaudy afternoon light, but she thought his blue eyes had some slight human warmth, and he was his usual well-mannered self.

"I'll take care of the car, Jess. Bethany, get your mother to her room. That infernal nurse is off duty, and I can't locate her. Robin has your mother's medication ready."

"You're the one who needs — oh, never mind!" Jess got out and went into the house with Bethy. It was surprisingly difficult to navigate the narrow back stairs. She understood for the first time what her doctors had meant about avoiding staircases and sleeping on the first floor. Advice she had chosen to ignore.

With the help of efficient Bethany and a frantic, anxious Robin, Jess obediently took her capsule and lay down. She had been partly right about her condition, however, and was feeling far better than the family thought when Chris and the children came tiptoeing in at dusk. Supposing her to be asleep, they argued in whispers about the day's events.

She heard Chris saying in a strained way, "They were together for hours. Hours! It had to be politics. What else could it be, knowing your mother?"

"Well, it wasn't any love-in!" Robin insisted with a furious indignation that his mother had not thought him capable of. He was almost as excited over his mother's reputation as he might be over the right to close off a Berkeley street.

"Be quiet! You'll wake her," his father whispered nervously, with a warning look in Jessica's direction. He sounded so very concerned that Jess found herself praying there was something more to his concern than the fulfillment of his political ambitions.

"Anyway," Bethany said in a loud whisper, "I happen to know Mom met Bick for another reason entirely. Father, you were right. It was political. She's been trying to help poor Mr. Alvaro. They're framing him. And thanks to Mom, now they know who —"

"Bethany!"

Alarmed, they all stared at Jess as she scrambled to sit up in bed. She realized belatedly how dangerous had been her betrayal of the Alvaro plans to Bethy who, like her mother, was apt to talk too much. Chris took two long steps that brought him beside the bed. With what appeared to be an effort, he retained that calm, unemotional front he had presented to the world and his family for eighteen years. He took Jessica's hand but his own fingers seemed cold and stiff, nervous to the touch.

Robin made an incoherent interruption, "Mother, take it easy now."

His father cut in. "Don't try to talk, dear. You've been overdoing." He seemed to feel the double meaning in this as her gaze flashed to his to see if he understood what he had said. He did not go on. His weakness at such a moment was a painful jolt to her, reminding Jess of the all-too-brief times in their life together when he had been so troubled, always politically, that he turned to her for comfort. She made some physical effort and smiled at him.

"Don't worry. Nothing is going to happen before the convention. I won't commit any indiscretions that will ruin your chances."

His cold fingers tightened over hers. He asked in a sharp voice that was curiously off-key, "Why? Is your life scheduled with such care?"

"Senator March's life? Or mine?"

He studied her. She felt a pulse beating heavily in her throat. She could not suppose his own passions were as deeply involved. He spoke to the children without really looking at them. The gesture was so like the old, typical Chris March that it hardened all her resolution to tell him the truth about their life together.

"Bethany, Robin . . . run along. Your mother wants to rest."

Robin nodded, and though Bethy was mumbling vague protests that "*she* wanted to talk to Mom," her brother took her by the elbow and propelled her out of the room.

The silence after the door closed was eery to Jess. Now that the real moment of the encounter had arrived she dreaded it, wanting in the most cowardly way to put it off. In his old, normal voice, Chris moved smoothly into that silence.

"Is it true, Jessica?"

"You mean, is it true that I've been unfaithful? An old-fashioned phrase, but perfectly descriptive."

"Is it? Descriptive of the truth, I mean?"

That sounded less calm. She freed her hand from his. She found the stiffness of his grasp contagious along with the cold, and exercised her fingers while she said straight out, "No. Not yet. Chris?" She stared up at him until he reddened, embarrassed or in some way emotionally involved. "Chris, I knew Bick Haldean before I ever knew you, but I loved you and I married you. That was a long time ago. I waited eighteen years for you to love me, only a little, but just as much as it was in you to love anything except your career." He winced but she was already lashing out with the final bitter weapon. "Bick loves me a little too . . . and he doesn't have to be bribed to love me."

That shook him. "Bribed? I suppose that means something. You're trying to destroy a good marriage. There has hardly been a harsh word or disagreement between us in all those eighteen years. How can you do this thing now, talk of the failure of our relationship? Unless it is because you are ill. You simply haven't been thinking like your old self. You've been a very sick woman."

Maybe he doesn't know, she thought. Maybe the whole "dowry" was something between Augusta March and Thea Souza. God! Make it so!

"I'm not ill. Not that way. And I know, all right. My heart may not be perfect but my head is just fine. Chris, what I meant —"

The telephone, with its seesaw ringing, cut her short. At the same time there was an abrupt and very feminine series of knocks on the door, followed by Sue Lyburg's voice. "Senator Chris? Washington is on the senator's line."

That did it. He got up from the bed with one jolting motion and strode toward the door.

"Have the call transferred to my study. No! I'll be with you in a second. Is it Herb Millvale?"

The next minute he was gone from the room and on his way out. Jess smiled wryly at the idea of transferring a call from the President of the United States, or of making his number one man wait on the line. Poor Chris! What a dilemma! Far more important than his relations with his erring wife.

Jessica sat up studying the phone. She knew that when Chris refused to have the call transferred, he must take the call on the extension in her den, and as she watched the telephone, the ringing stopped. By a movement so swift she surprised herself, she took the telephone off its cradle. Herb Millvale was just beginning to speak to Chris.

"Millvale here. It's not a nice bit, Chris. Just wanted to give you the signals as I read 'em. The president feels we have to check out any dirt. Make sure the mud doesn't stick, you know."

"What mud? I don't understand. Look,

Herb. Does The Man appear to take any stock in it?"

"Not for me to say. It's a matter of checking it out."

Jessica guessed that President Walters was present in the room with Millvale, which would explain his caution. Apparently, Chris understood as well. He asked in what, for Chris, was an unusually abrupt voice, "Let me talk to The Man. This is bound to be some smear — probably started by that radical Alvaro and his gang. They know my stand against all their violent tactics."

"Sure, Chris, sure. Bound to be. The president has just taken time out of a real douzy day to see a couple of visitors who —" There was a disturbance on the line and Jess suspected the President had cut Millvale short. "Anyway," Millvale went on in some confusion, "he's only got a minute, but here he is."

The suave, familiar tones of President Walters flowed over the line. "Evening, Christopher. How's the boy?"

Jessica could imagine Chris's anxiety over this chit-chat.

"Fine, Mr. President. Just fine. I — ah — Herb says you're busy as a hound — that is, very busy."

"My boy, this job is always busier than a

hound-dog. I called to find out especially how that pretty little wife of yours is coming along."

There was clearly astonishment in Chris's voice. "Coming along? But she's in excellent condition. That is to say, she's been making frequent appearances at luncheons, political gatherings, women's clubs. Only yesterday she was in San Francisco at a . . ."

"Yes, my boy?"

"A political luncheon."

But the pause had been bad. Jess felt the doubt betrayed in it.

President Walters's unctuous quality came through loud and clear.

"Good to hear. Very good to hear. It makes a liar out of my informants. All I wanted to know, Christopher. So go back to writing your acceptance speech and — oh yes." A chuckle. "Keep your nose clean. No gossip. Not a word. Nothing that could even look like a smear. You understand?"

"No! Just a minute, Mr. President? Who told you my wife was still sick?"

"Not still sick, my boy. Far from it! A little too well, you might say. However, give my love to our favorite senator."

"Yes sir. But —"

"Good night, Christopher." There was one distant click but it seemed a very long time before Chris hung up. Jessica could feel his nervousness, the uncertainty and knew this sort of maddening mystery would give Chris one of his bad nights. He would get something he called "tension headaches" and take an assortment of pills and capsules, none of which would help because the causes of these headaches were the real crises of her husband's life.

"I've probably seen the last of him for tonight."

She began to wonder if Chris would entirely forget that he had left things between his wife and himself at a stage approaching divorce. She was wrong in this, however. Chris came back almost immediately and with the logical question.

"Jess, this is vitally important. The Man has been getting some smears about us. You see now, what harm these little crotchets of yours can cause. All this ridiculous business about our marriage being imperfect and the rest of it. I've called D.D. He's got to find out where this smear is coming from."

She groaned. "Not Dominik. Sometimes I get the feeling I'm married to that grinning Cheshire cat."

"Sometimes," he threw at her from left field, "you get the feeling you are married to anyone but me."

She immediately used this to return to the point which seemed all important to her. "That would be adultery, and you apparently believe I couldn't inspire that kind of love."

"Not you, Jess. I know you too well. And it's as Bethany said, you kissed that fellow the minute you saw us. I don't pretend to know the ways of a woman's mind, but I do know you. You've always been faithful to me." He leaned over the bed and kissed her on the forehead. Under the caress, maddening because it was always successful, Jess made a face.

"Look here, Chris, this passionate belief of yours in my innocence is —" Then she took a deep, cutting breath. "All right. I confess it. I didn't drive off with Bick to make love to him. You can reassure Bethy; I know she still has doubts. She's infatuated with him." Surely the most wildly enraging thing about her supposed love affair with Bick was that Chris had so easily been convinced of her innocence — or her lack of attraction.

But he was already deep in his own plans. "I've got to make some sort of appearance on that TV news show in Sacramento tomorrow. This is the time, Jess. We make the appearance together and give them a lead-in to ask about any stories they're sitting on. Like your support of Alvaro. Just a denial will do.

A sympathetic denial. You think what happened about the bomb and all is appalling and you aren't making any wild judgments until all the facts are in. That will get you off the hook." He went on with the other campaign issues while she opened her mouth several times but got nothing out. In spite of everything, she found herself delighting in this old Chris, with his enthusiasm, his vigorous plans, all the selfish qualities and processes of thought that combined to make him the man she had loved.

She looked at him as he talked, but she did not listen. She kept asking him silently: Did you have to be bribed to marry me, to sleep with me, to make love, to produce Robin and Bethy? Was it all done for that *dowry?* When he stopped for breath she began decisively, "Chris, I want to talk to you about us . . . about what made you marry me."

"Yes, yes, dear. We'll put that aside until bedtime. Shall we? Then I'll tell you — no, I'll *show* you what made me marry you. Meanwhile, that sounds like D.D. in the driveway. You will be nice to old Dex, won't you? His whole life is wrapped up in the Marches."

"In the Marches' careers, at any rate."

But he had gone to the windows and pushed them open. He leaned out far enough to see the garage and driveway along the side of the house. "That you, Dex? I'm up here. Come on in."

"I see more of him than I do of my own children," she remarked crossly.

On his way to the door he chided her with a little smile, "Careful, dear. You are beginning to sound like a shrew. You mustn't let your recent illness get you down. You really are looking much healthier these days." He paused, added what for Chris was an extravagently sensual remark, "You were looking so good today when Bethany and I saw you, that you made me damnably jealous, if you want to know the truth."

But not looking good enough, apparently, to make him retain that jealousy. He was insultingly unsuspicious, but Jess soon found that Dexter Dominik made up for this particular way in which her husband was remiss. The campaign manager met Chris on the stairs and Jess, unable to contain her curiosity, got up and went out in the hall to join them. She felt a trifle dizzy going down the stairs, but rather agreed with D.D.'s suggestion that "a nice frosty martini with a twist will fix you up."

They went into one corner of the austere, empire salon and Jess found herself senselessly annoyed when Sue Lyburg, instead of the usual maid, Mary-Claire, brought in the drinks. There was, of course, an extra cocktail for Sue whose presence, D.D. said, would be essential.

"She may be needed, in case we want to have anything transcribed for future reference. Now, then. Everybody set?"

Chris cut in anxiously, "Who do you think is responsible for the smear about Jessica?"

D.D. tapped his white teeth with his thumbnail. He was not looking at Jess but she felt his dislike, his resentment at her "indiscretion," the recent visits to the city which had given credence to the smear.

"I think the problem at the moment is to cancel out the harmful effects of the business. We've got to keep in mind at all times that it *is* a smear. That's the way to think: a smear." Chris raised his head abruptly, an indication to Jess that he understood the none-too-subtle hint in D.D.'s bland assurance. "Kayo, then. We meet it head on, with daily appearances together, oftener if possible — and play it cozy, for God's sake!"

"I'm due for that Sacramento news show tomorrow," Chris put in. "If Jessica is feeling well, she'll be with me."

"She damned well better be!"

Jessica and Chris stared at him, Jess sardonically amused, Chris indignant.

"Now, see here, Dex! What is that supposed to mean?"

Jess was contemptuous of D.D.'s double trick, his legitimate efforts to further Chris's career, along with his now-overt dislike of Jess. He must always have wished that Chris were married to a woman more suited to the artificial life of a politician in the national limelight. She calmed Chris with a hand on his arm.

"He's right, Chris, about the smear. I was actually in San Francisco on quite another matter. You might call it a political matter. But either way, the name of the game for us is compatibility."

D.D.'s rocketing eyebrows went up higher. "Bravo, Mrs. — ah — Senator March! Compatibility is the keynote — and a bit of warmth between you, the little tricks of affection the women go for, these are all vital."

"Fine. Fine!" Chris cut him off sharply, with a new impatience. He surprised Jess by swallowing his drink in one long gulp. "There is nothing to the preposterous smear anyway, so forget that. It's simply a foul dig at my Jess." She flushed at the unusual endearment, but she almost believed it because it was so unlike Chris. However, being Chris, he went on: "What trash they spread about her is not im-

244

portant. The important thing is to find out *who* is spreading the smear."

That produced an idea simultaneously between Chris and D.D. while Jessica sipped her martini and listened with what was, for her, detachment. For eighteen years her husband's problems had been hers, his panic affected her, his despair sickened her with sympathy for him. But when she felt the familiar nervous stomach, the pulse pounding in her throat fit to choke her, she reminded herself that neither Chris nor his evil genius cared nearly as much about her own possible wrongdoing as they did about the identity of the president's informant. They hit on Juan Alvaro's people for reasons that escaped Jess who said abruptly, "I personally would elect the Duvauxs or the new owners of the Croisetti Farms. That Puddles woman —" She broke off, wishing she had kept quiet and let them fight it out.

D.D. looked into his glass. "Sue, baby, how about a refill for senator Jess and for Chris here?"

Then, when Jess breathed calmly again, deciding he had not noticed her slip, D.D. swung around with every tooth shining as he smiled at her. "She's quite a talker, that Puddles Clormann. But what made you think Puddles could reach The Man?

Or even Herb Millvale?"

The idea of D.D. in juxtaposition to Puddles Clormann seemed to burst in Jessica's tired brain. She got up so quickly she spilled the last of her cocktail on the spotless Aubusson carpet.

"Dex, you were there in the Gold Room Bar the day I had my heart attack."

"Naughty-naughty, Jess. Nervous exhaustion we call it. Remember?"

"Never mind that. You were there, and you heard Puddles bragging about the . . . execution, they called it." She took a hard, painful breath. *"You were the man whose voice I remember."*

Chris looked at them, puzzled and uneasy. "What is all this? What man? What execution are you talking about?"

For a span of seconds they had been oblivious to him. An old bond, forged in personal dislike and reinforced by this open enmity, held them together. Jessica did not look at Chris as she said with a kind of bitter triumph, "He knew about the plot all the time, didn't you, Dex?"

Chris surprised her by jumping into the breach. "Don't be silly, Jess! Dex was at that bar to take care of you with the press that day. Don't you remember any of the details?"

Bethany was in the doorway motioning

to them, but Jess couldn't resist the topper to her husband's remark, "I am beginning to remember a surprising amount of the details. What is it, Bethy?"

"Turn on the TV, the Westlake show," the girl snapped, looking so very fiery eyed she startled Jessica who got up and went over to her while D.D. and Chris made a dive for the big console set in an obscure corner.

"Bethy, are you all right? What is it?"

"Me, Mother? I'm great." That word "Mother" was the tip-off.

"Are you angry with me?"

Bethy's lips twisted as if she wanted to cry but remembered she was a big girl now. "It's true, isn't it? I called Bick. I apologized for the way Father and I got all upset over you kissing him. And he said — he said — he kissed *you*. He said he loved you." Her voice broke in spite of her efforts, and she angrily wiped the tears away. "How could you do it, Mother? How could you take him away from me!"

Jess attempted to put an arm around Bethany, her brain tiredly putting words together, to make the girl understand the precise feeling Bick had for Bethy. The tenderness, and fatherly, even comradely quality. But Bethy was too emotionally involved for mature reasoning.

"I don't believe it! You must have told him I was too young."

"I told him nothing of the sort. You must remember, Bethy, I knew Bick long before you were born."

"Don't remind me! I'm going to see him tomorrow whether you like it or not. I'm going down the San Joaquin to that boycott meeting, and make him tell me how he really feels."

"We'll talk about that tomorrow," Jess said more firmly than she felt. As there was no reasoning with Bethany in this mood, she went back across the long room to join the two men at the television set. They were both agitated to the point of total silence at what they saw. Immediately Jess understood the reason for their agitation.

The Washington section of the news program was devoted to an interview with certain of the day's visitors to the White House, and there before the cameras, oozing ingratiating charm, stood Governor and Mrs. Simeon McClatchey.

Jess found her voice before the men did. "They must have used rockets to get there so soon. They were in this room last night."

"That treacherous bastard," D.D. muttered, "sold out his benefactor!"

Chris remarked wearily, "At least we know

where the smear came from. Sim hot-footed it to Washington on a midnight flight, just to get the knife into me with The Man." He turned to Jessica. "Dear, this is a real blow, you know that. It means you've got to be before the public every possible minute. Reminding them that Sim's filth is just that: a smear."

"Before the public together," Dex put in. "No more running off to give lip service to that radical wine fellow. Nothing that suggests any kind of break between you — physically or politically. And as for you, Chris: no more coddling your wife on the grounds of health."

"Now, see here!" Chris began, but D.D. waved aside any such gallantry.

"Both of you must realize you are within an inch of losing the nomination. Your only real chance is to make a liar out of Sim McClatchey. The Marches think alike. They work for the same goals. There isn't a breath of scandal. *And no ill-health talk!*"

Jessica looked down at her hands, avoiding her husband. She didn't want to see the spectacle of his crawling for an office goaded on by a man like Dex who had countenanced murder.

But she could not avoid hearing it.

"We know," Chris mumbled. "We both understand."

– FOURTEEN –

In spite of all Chris's clear determination to be a good husband that night and more especially, to blot out with his love-making his wife's memories of Bick Haldean, Jess ruined the project by harping on Dex. She sat at her dressing table brushing her hair and emphasizing her condemnation of the man by harsh brush strokes.

"The man is little better than a murderer, Chris. Don't you understand? I'm convinced he heard everything I heard that day in the Gold Room, and he could have warned the Alvaros. That union business agent was blown to pieces because I forgot what I heard and D.D. knew but didn't want to stop it!"

Chris, in his pajama bottoms, with the top thrown jauntily over his shoulder, had been huddled in front of Jessica's portable TV in her room, hoping to catch a new clue to the McClatcheys' betrayal on the late news. He turned the television off impatiently, saying, "I wish you wouldn't talk like this about Dex, even if you are half-joking. These are days when we've got to be particularly careful. Every word has to be weighed. A slip can cost us the nomination. You know how The Man is about the slightest hint of scandal."

"He probably wouldn't consider a passive support to a murder as anything scandalous, dear, so don't give it another thought."

His head went up quickly at her tone. "We haven't finished discussing what you call 'our own problems.' I didn't mean to cut you off tonight, but so many important things came up, I guess we got sidetracked."

She smiled at the kind of thing he considered more important than their marriage and, because she knew there was no hope that he would understand, she shrugged.

"We'll wait until after the campaign. I can hold out that long."

He stopped by her chair, leaned over the crown of her head and looked into the mirror with her.

"Pretty handsome couple, I'd say. Don't tease me, and yourself, by talking about problems, dear. Problems are for other marriages, not ours."

Expressionless, she studied him in the mirror and knew he really believed his own words. Even after seeing her in Bick's arms, he was determined to believe in their perfect marriage — not because he loved and trusted her, but because any absence of belief would destroy him politically.

"Chris, kiss me and say good night. We don't have to prove we're the ideal couple in the bedroom. Though I'm sure D.D. will get to that eventually."

He looked surprisingly hurt as he left her, and she wondered if his vanity, or just possibly his heart had been wounded. She found it extraordinarily difficult to sleep and had to get up in the night and take a capsule. She kept dreaming she was running on a dark highway with Robin and Bethy, and there in the distance, were two men, each offering her an assisting hand to help her off that endless road. It was so ridiculous, so obvious a symbol that she woke herself up in a turmoil of indecision.

"Don't be silly!" she told herself with enough stern assurance to shake off the mood.

Finding her awake at 7:10, Chris came in fully dressed and carrying a tray of coffee and her prebreakfast indigestion pill.

"Very unromantic," she murmured at sight of the tiny white pill, but as Chris kissed her and she kissed him back, only partly from habit, she had to explain, "The pill, I mean."

He patted her hand and offered her the glass of water which, unfortunately, was lukewarm. After she had conquered her first impatience with his anxiety to get going, she laughed, and Chris sat down hopefully on the edge of the bed.

"Feel better today?"

Innocently she said, "Fine."

"Good. That Sacramento interview is scheduled for noon sharp, and it's live. I thought we might make a brief appearance at the airport first. You know. All the usual schmaltz, as Dex calls it. And then, D.D. has several very short appearances lined up for the afternoon."

She yawned, drank coffee too heavily laced with milk, and inquired with distaste, "Which airport?"

"Ah — both."

She winced but did not deny him. She had made up her mind to help him in every way until the nomination and the election. Afterward, always assuming he won, she would make plans for her future, whatever that might be. In any event, it would be made with the opinions and preferences of the children heavily weighed. Often, as in her dreams, she was not sure whether Bick Haldean *was* her future. Although Robin and Bethy were nearly grown, they still needed her. In some ways, despite their father's single-minded pursuit of his ambition, it was quite probable they needed Chris too.

Jess felt a little tired that morning after the

itinerary for the day was explained by Chris, but this was something she should have expected. There was the annoying short flight to Sacramento which would be hot as hades this time of year, and the appearances everywhere that must be staged with unnaturally devoted caresses and attentions between her and Chris, and the luncheons; there were sure to be several luncheons laced with several cocktail gatherings. And preluncheon cocktail parties nowadays had a bad habit of bringing to her mind that other cocktail party where the assassination of a man was openly discussed. She even wondered if, in some terrible way, she and her family might suffer because they used and were used by a man like Dexter Dominik. The longer she thought about it, the more she was convinced that she had been right in her suspicion: D.D. had certainly known as much as she herself did, and more, about the planned murder of Juan Alvaro.

While drinking her coffee, which had unfortunately cooled off, she wondered if D.D. possibly knew of any other plan in the offing, some plot to take the place of that hideous business at Alvaro's house near Sonoma. With this thought behind all her movements during the next few hours, Jess dressed in her newest suit whose tailored lines were carefully softened and feminized by the frilled and transparent blouse. She had often wanted to wear the maddest new St. Laurent pants suit, or the Courrèges boots, or a Gernreich see-through swimsuit, but Chris March's ambition was the great barrier. His wife must always be neatly, but not too fashionably, middle class. Like a label for a carefully conservative liberal.

Robin made a tousled appearance shortly afterward to steal some of her decaffinated coffee, but though Jess was especially concerned over Bethy, the girl seemed determined to sulk in bed. When Jess and Chris came in to kiss her good-bye, she was still mutinous. Though she allowed them to kiss her exposed cheek, she had nothing to say. For the thousandth time in his life as a father, Chris murmured, "I simply don't understand that child!"

One of the very busy, very efficient young men from Chris March's Washington office got him and Jess to the plane on time in spite of delays for a local television news service which hinted, while picturing "the loving pair," that there was already gossip abroad about Senator Jessica. Chris had smiled broadly, put his arm around Jess and pulled her close.

"Does this look like there is trouble between my Jess and me?"

The first time he had called her "his Jess" long ago, she had cried, she loved it so much.

She tried that hot morning at the airport and almost succeeded in feeling something of that first miracle.

She was displeased, though not surprised to see Dexter Dominik on the field and used the few moments before the Sacramento plane took off to be pleasant to him, beating around the bush but getting closer to the thing she wanted to find out: was there another plot against the Alvaros, and did Dex know of its details?

D.D. seemed disarmed by the time they were boarding, and Chris was puzzled at the easy cameraderie between his wife and his friend. But though Jess played it cool, in her children's words, she could get nothing definite out of her hints that she was having a change of heart over the whole civil-rights problem, particularly as it involved her husband's Mexican-American constituents. She held tight to her husband's arm and looked at him adoringly for the cameras, and agreed publicly with everything he said, but she was herself again a minute later as they went up the steps to the plane.

"In spite of everything, I'd be willing to bet that the Alvaro forces will throw a monkey wrench into your plans to starve them out. They may even lose the election. He's a charming man, but from what you and Dex say, he can be very dangerous."

D.D. was looking out the window, counting the crowd with Marcher placards by the time he answered her comment, laughing as he said absently, "Forget it, senator. That's one problem you can cancel out. Chris, this was a bigger crowd by at least a hundred than the one that met Sim when he came back from the Mexico conference."

"Good God! I hope so. Sim couldn't draw my crowd if his life depended on it."

Jess mentioned Alvaro's name once more a few minutes later but learned nothing specific except the alarming fact that mention of the organizer's name roused D.D. and her husband to exchange quick glances of mutual understanding. Was it possible Chris knew something about a new attack on Alvaro and his union?

By the time the jet was on the field in the state capital, however, Chris, and especially Dex, had a great deal more to think about than trying to keep Jessica off a forbidden topic. There was a far-bigger crowd than they had expected and D.D.'s first reaction was jubilant.

"How's that for a weekday crowd, and before the conventions, at that!" He was still raving while Jessica, with apparently sharper eyes, read a message printed across a bedsheet and held up against the hot, still Sacramento sky by four youngsters a little older than Robin:

CHRIS AND JESS — SELLOUTS!

"What damned impudence!" Chris exclaimed having seen the big sign. He tried to recover his composure and smiled faintly. "They used to say my image was too urbane and too formal. Now, I see I'm bad old Chris. The least they could do, though, is show some respect to Jessica."

That was just a sampling of the unpleasantness. By the time they reached the field themselves, Chris and Jessica found that though they were surrounded by their own clique, the nucleus of the March workers, there were others, a surprising number of Mexican descent, Negroes, and teen-agers behind the Marchers who called out:

"How's your love life, Jess?"

"Hey, Jess! You gettin' the newspapers to sell out too? That why you so chummy with newsmen?"

And sometimes there was a plaintive:

"Senator Chris! Why you betray the Mexican-Americans? What happen to you?"

Chris turned distinctly red and muttered to Jessica "How can you answer poor devils like that last one? They don't understand. They can't see I'm on their side. I've always been on their side."

Jessica thought, he believes it. Poor Chris! After nearly eighteen years in politics he still believes everything he says. And it occurred to her ironically that "Poor Chris" was lucky. He never seemed to have any self-doubts. The other guy was always wrong.

Meanwhile, D.D. was exchanging muttered and slightly desperate comments with the capital's most important lobbyist, who also happened to be the organizer of the Sacramento Marchers. Jessica guessed they were even more surprised and confused than she was. Her fast-paced impetus brought Chris along too, but she saw that he was a great deal more shocked than she was by this unexpected hatred of the crowd, and he cared a great deal more. In an odd sort of way, she admired him for his naïve disappointment in the fickle mob.

Jessica smiled, more or less mechanically, and kept on smiling when something spattered over her body, about shoulder high, and she realized it had been a whole cluster of purple grapes.

Damn! she thought. I'll never get the stain out. She wished she hadn't worn her new gray knit suit today. It was the worst possible material and color for stains. She kept her mind firmly on trivialities, like this stain-removal job ahead. It made the whole horrible episode bearable.

Chris had been seeking out friendly faces in the crowd, calling, waving with his free hand, the other carefully and publicly around his wife's trim waist, and Jess knew the whole business might throw him off his normally cool stride, but D.D. was watching him with a care and disapproval that secretly angered Jessica. She wondered if, in just such a moment one day, he might scratch Chris off his list of clients and sell him out.

When one of the boys with a stringy blond beard popped up in front of them, Chris was so shaken he cried out, "Robin! For God's sake!" Belatedly, he realized the lanky youth merely looked like Robin before his son had been persuaded to shave.

The walk through this noisy crowd of mixed Marchers and hecklers lasted less than two minutes. The shortness of the lapsed time startled Jessica when they had gone through the airport to the waiting limousine and she glanced at her watch. D.D. had signaled certain Sacramento dignitaries who witnessed what they called the Marches' "indignities" and there were repeated apologies which involved Chris whom they addressed. Jess blamed herself for her selfishness but couldn't seem to concentrate on anything except the grape stains and the nasty feeling of an egg — fortunately not rotten — which dripped down, bits of shell and all, over the calf of her left leg.

She told herself that it was ridiculous, in the face of this trouble, to sympathize with that riotous crowd, but whatever excuses Chris might make for his own behavior during his career, she knew perfectly well they were right about her. So far as her personal beliefs were concerned, she had been behaving this morning very like a sell-out. She knew her deepest convictions were on the side of the grape- and wine-workers, and she was not behaving very much like that at the moment.

When the men looked at her, expecting her answer to something they had asked and which she hadn't heard, she apologized with an attempt at good humor, "I didn't know eggs were so sticky. They seem to cling to my legs."

"My wife should never have been subjected to this outrage!" Chris cut in furiously. "She's simply a tool in all this. They've no right —"

"Cut it!" D.D. interrupted with a decisiveness that angered Jess as much as the egg-and-grape throwing had done. "The minute Sim McClatchey appointed her Senator to fill out your term, she became as much a target as you are. Be reasonable, Chris."

Because she was angry with D.D. in any case, and it seemed doubly stupid to stand here beside the car arguing, Jess called to both of them, ignoring the apologetic committee, "Get in the car, for God's sake! We'll be late at the television studio, and I've got to change these damned stockings."

Without another word, Chris got in beside her, Dex squeezing in on her other side and two capital men taking the jump seats. Chris looked tense and stiff but he took Jess's hand and twisted it unconsciously until she winced.

He said, misunderstanding her mood, "It is disgusting, dear, but don't worry. They'll be made to apologize. You'll see."

"Never mind," she said wearily. "Don't bother." She felt extraordinarily tired, and when they started off with a sharp jolt, she fell against Chris. He was studying her worriedly but she did not feel like reassuring him. She was simply too tired.

Although someone gave her nylons to exchange for her own ruined ones, and the grape stains were sponged rather inexpertly off her suit, she never afterward recalled what she and Chris said on the noon television program except that people looked less worried after the show than before. Afterward she murmured more firmly than she felt to Chris,

"We must have done something right, anyway."

But what she was really thinking about was D.D.'s obliging reassurance to her and to Chris as they sat down under the blinding television lights: "Take my word, you can forget the whole union deal after tonight. They'll be a snake without its head, the fangs removed. They're back of this whole cruddy deal at the airport. Sim's gossip started their lies. Well there'll be no more of that after tonight."

Anxiously Jessica whispered during the commercial, "Chris, what is going on tonight? What's he talking about?"

"I don't know. Don't talk about it now, Jess."

She gave up. She felt her own weakness, her cowardice, but here was Chris in bad trouble with unexpected riots and betrayals, and her heart, if not her head, told her she had to think of his welfare before she considered the problems of a comparative stranger named Juan Alvaro.

After the noon show, the Marches were escorted to the inevitable cocktails and luncheon where the grape stains on Jess's suit served as a lever, a weapon with which the luncheon guests, chiefly female, could lash out at "The Enemy" who, in this case, was not the opposite political party but the aggregate farm laborers and migratory workers with their defending champion, Juan Alvaro.

It became successively more boring and distasteful as the day and the luncheon wore on. Sometime late in the afternoon during the third cocktail party, where Jess was lethargically sipping bitter lemon over ice, the female head of Sacramento Marchers came hurrying across the room to her.

"Senator, there seems to be an important phone call for you."

"For me? Not for my husband?" Jess asked surprised.

"The young man specifically asked for Mrs. March."

The words "young man" made her think suddenly of Robin. She got up hurriedly and stepped into the alcove to get the extension phone. In politics she had learned that no one was above listening in. She had done so herself.

It was Robin. "Mother, I had a hell of a time getting you. An old bi — dame has been calling you all day. I touted her off, but the last time she called I got to thinking, and I decided to let you in on it. Then, if you want to give her the heave-ho, it's your business. What d'you say?"

"Yes, fine. Who was it, Robin? What did she say?" For some reason Jess had a picture of Elena Alvaro calling for help, and she felt as guilty as if she had kicked someone in the stomach.

"It's that Gladys Duvaux — a real crawlie. She says — no cliché-dropper she! — that it's a matter of life and death."

"Robin! Never mind the clichés. What else did she say?" She paused and added more plaintively, "Dear, I'm glad to hear from you, but things are pretty tense here today; so please don't make jokes. Mrs. Duvaux called? What was it about?"

An instant later she was sorry she had been so abrupt with him. His voice was distinctly subdued.

"She didn't say, but she left a couple of numbers. Have you got a pencil handy, Mother?"

She got out a little gold ball-point pen and one of the psychedelic notebooks Bethy gave her from Takahashi's. "Okay, Robin, shoot." She scrawled the two numbers, one of which was Gladys Duvaux's private phone and the other the Duvaux household number. "Robin? Did she say why it was life and death?"

"No, Mom. You know those old rattle-brains. Say, do you think it's really that important? I mean, something —"

"Life and death? I wish I knew. Your father

and I may be a little late for dinner. Take care of your sister and if you can't wait, have dinner at the usual time, dear."

"Take care of my sister!" You've got to be kidding, Mom! Bethy goes her way. I can't stop her — like now. She's off to join that big wing-ding with Bick Haldean, down at Bolano in the valley. Well, keep cool Mother . . . and Father too."

Jess groaned at Bethany's willfulness, but trusted to luck and Bick to take care of her. "Do the best you can until we get home. I'm awfully sorry we have to leave you alone so much these days, but you know how anxious your father is about the coming convention, and things haven't looked too good today." Full of guilt and torn by her duties as wife and as mother, she added anxiously, "You do understand, don't you, dear?"

After breezily telling her not to worry about him, Robin hung up leaving Jess more uneasy than ever. She put a call through to Gladys Duvaux's private number and was surprised at Mrs. Duvaux's quick answer.

"Jessica? My God, I've been nearly out of my mind!" Gladys Duvaux's bubbling voice sounded hushed, yet panic-stricken. She appeared to be talking directly into the phone.

"Mrs. Duvaux! Are you all right? What is it? Don't you want to talk to my husband?"

"No, No! He probably knows the whole thing, like Earl. Don't tell Chris March about it, for Lord's sake! Jessica dear, they're going to blow him up tonight. Down at that place in the San Joaquin. After their stupid meeting."

It was like a needle-sharp spray chilling Jess. She was squeezing the phone so hard, she felt the pain of the pressure in her fingertips. She knew at once it was Juan Alvaro's murder that was planned, but she asked with a stern pretense at calm, "How did you find out?"

"I heard Earl talking to that Puddles Clormann's dreadful husband. They're like gangsters! Horrible! And then I discovered that Earl had known all along about that car being rigged to blow up at Alvaro's bungalow that day. My own husband sent me over to make peace with the Alvaros, and all the time he knew how dangerous it was going to be!"

Incredulous Jess glanced over her shoulder and then lowered her voice. "You can't mean that Mr. — your husband knew you would be hurt."

"Well . . . he warned me not to go near the car, he said it would be bad for our image. But I got my face scratched by flying glass — and I still have a bandage on my neck."

"But are you sure about tonight?" The woman must be sure. There was a terrible certainty about this along side of D.D.'s hints about tonight.

"I tell you, I heard that awful eastern man, right in Earl's study. One of the new Croisetti owners. Earl didn't seem to like it. He kept saying 'don't tell me. I don't want to know.'"

With an enormous effort, Jess asked after a quick, painful breath, "Did you get the particulars? How is it to be done? *I must know!*"

"I don't know, and neither does Earl, I'm sure. Jessica? What an appalling thing! We all used to talk about this sort of thing. But I didn't honestly think they meant it. And that sweet Elena Alvaro! I'd hate to have her blown up. Or all those young teen-agers who will be down at Bolano tonight. They always crowd around —"

Jess cried hoarsely, "Dear God, no!" She thought for one ghastly moment that she would faint. Then she pulled herself together and asked, "Haven't you any more facts at all?"

"That's all. I'm sorry."

Jess hung up on the still-chattering woman.

Bethy! Wild, well-meaning little Bethy! She would be one of those teen-agers crowding around the Alvaros tonight!

– FIFTEEN –

Chris looked shaken but his voice was stronger than Jessica remembered in many years.

"A plane is impossible at this hour — and there isn't an airport near Bolano. We'll have the police car and siren. And the sheriff's office in Bolano County will be on the lookout; they have pictures of Bethany from the last campaign."

"They've got to find her, Chris. They've got to!"

He put an arm around her as they walked rapidly, not quite running, down the steps to the car at the curb.

"Now, don't panic. It'll all be over . . . all safe and sound in a couple of hours. D.D doesn't know any of the facts about tonight, just that something is going to happen. I had no idea it was to be something like — this."

She thought he might have suspected more and simply kept his eyes closed, but she desperately wanted to believe in him now. She herself was so weak with fear for Bethy that she stumbled on the bottom step, and only his arm kept her from falling.

"If we could have reached Bick before he

left! He'd find Bethy. Or at the very least, he'd track down that Clormann crowd."

"I'm sure he would. He's quite a paragon!"

She thought he sounded jealous, but it may have been his natural display of nerves during these harrowing minutes. Once she would have been embarrassed to step into a police car with uniformed escort and siren, but after years of rushing from one political hustings to another, she was no longer embarrassed and her only concern on this stifling hot evening was to reach Bolano in the quickest possible time.

The car started off with the roar of a high-powered motor and she clutched her own shoulders, hunching forward as if she could give the car an extra push. Beside her, sitting straight and rather stiff, Chris watched her with concern.

"You mustn't worry like this. It's bad for you, dear. The sheriff's office down there will locate the baby long before we get there."

It was an age since he had called Bethany "the baby," and for some reason she began to cry, silently, hiding her head between her arms. She felt better that way, less sick and dizzy. The men in the front seat began to run the nerve-wracking siren. Chris, whose life had been so carefully and precisely timed that it left him little room for emotion, suddenly raised his hand to his head and Jess, glancing up more or less indifferently, saw that his hand was shaking. He smiled at her faintly.

"Got a headache."

From long habit she felt the old concern and solicitude.

"Chris! I'm so sorry. I have some aspirin here in my bag somewhere . . . a little gold pillbox. Where the devil is it?"

"It won't do any good, I'm afraid. No water."

Their attention was caught by the voices of the policemen in the front seat. The siren had stopped, and the officer in front of Jess was handling messages from headquarters. She and Chris listened anxiously. The sheriff's men in Bolano had not yet located Bethany, or the Alvaros, but at least they had talked with Bick Haldean who was now on the lookout.

While the two-way police report went on, Jessica breathed her first relieved breath and assured Chris, "Bick will find her. He's very —"

"I know!" Chris said shortly. He rubbed his forehead but for one of the few times in his life Jess thought the gesture was unconscious; he wasn't trying to impress anyone. He murmured, "I told her not to go. I'm not one of those modern, permissive parents. I laid down the law, didn't I? And yet she went right out. What gets into children these days?"

Jessica thought there was no point in reminding him that his image of himself as an old-fashioned father was tarnished by his absenteeism. Her own record on that score was nearly as bad. She had chosen her husband's needs over those of her children.

There was more garbled radio conversation in the front seat, talk of a mob of "hippies" and university students led by a couple of recognized troublemakers — whatever that meant — and of a probable conflict with the police. As nearly as Jessica could understand it, the "questionable characters" were marching to "protect" the meeting of Alvaro's migrant laborers which was to be held in a ploughed field. The belligerence would obviously be furnished by the conflict between this totally extraneous mob and the local police.

Chris groaned and shook his head. "A child of ours mixed up in that kind of thing!"

Jessica said suddenly, "I wonder if that's how it is to be done."

Chris didn't understand, but the officer in front of Jess looked over his shoulder at her. He looked grim.

"Lady, you got a point there. If there's a killing planned, and meant to be covered up, these hoodlums that lead the hippie march could do the job with nobody the wiser."

Much as Jess loathed brutality, by gangs or by police, she could see how a few dangerous men and women, planted among the innocent, head-in-the-clouds young people could shoot Alvaro and others in the scuffle. Such deaths would be laid either to the police or the hippies. The death of a child like Bethy would simply serve better to point up the bloodshed ingendered by Alvaro's organizers.

"Hurry! Can't you hurry?" she cried.

When the police car tore through the quiet, dusty town of Bolano, the main street still smoked with valley heat. They had gotten no news on the police radio for the last few miles, and when Chris reached out to take Jessica's hand, either to comfort her or to gain comfort, she did not know which of them was more cold, stiff, and frightened.

After a brief discussion with the local police captain who joined them in the tightly crowded front seat, shaking hands with "our senator and Mrs. Senator," they raced on, at Chris's instruction, to the out-of-town site of the meeting. The captain explained that from here on they were in county territory under Sheriff Bilkens's jurisdiction. It was easy for Jess to guess why he was anxious to delegate authority. Beyond the city limits and past two shabby motels, lay acres of ploughed fields, conspicuously treeless, bare, and hot with the valley's night heat. Normally deserted, they now gleamed with lights strung from trailers, U-hauls, campers, and temporary setups of huge spotlights.

"Looks like a gypsy camp," Chris muttered, looking around with Jess in the desperate hope of seeing their miniskirted daughter.

The siren had cut a way through swarms of men with some sidearms but mostly rifles, the regular sheriff's deputies reinforced by a local posse. They seemed to be waiting for some overt move by the crowd beyond that milled around like masquerade creatures, half-invisible. Jess made out men and women and a scattering of children, their faces now bright and gaudy in the spotlight, then sinister in the dark between the lights.

Before the car and its siren stopped a man was at the rear door forcing it open. Jessica, thinking they were about to be attacked, screamed, and Chris exclaimed furiously, "The first one in here will get my foot in his face!"

"Wait!" One of the spotlights shown on the car just as the officers got out to collar the man, and Jess nudged Chris frantically. "Don't you see who it is?" She scrambled to get out and fell into Bick Haldean's arms. "Oh,

Bick! Where is she? How is she?"

One of the officers put a heavy hand on Bick's shoulder but Chris, getting out of the car, interfered.

"No! He's a friend. Haldean, have you seen Bethany?"

"Not yet. She and the Alvaros took off before I got here. I'm told Mrs. Alvaro was looking out for her. Juan was going to meet privately with the head of that mob of juvenile storm troopers across the fields. He wanted to discourage them. Protest march, they call it. But not one is connected with Alvaro's people."

The police nodded to each other. "Sure. The kid's safe. It's this riff-raff'll give us the trouble." They spread out to join the sheriff and discuss ways and means of controlling the fight and protecting the Marches once the protest got under way.

Left behind in the dark back of the police car, Jessica and Chris figuratively clung to Bick in their hope.

"Then can't we go to these Alvaros and get our girl?" Chris asked as Bick pointed out to him a farmhouse huddling on the flat horizon.

"I tried to get across. I took a jeep around the south, but the damned fields are honeycombed with kids lying flat. You've got to kill them to get by. They insist they're protecting the Alvaros, but so far as I can see, they are simply holding them as hostages to insure the unionization of Alvaro's people. Their average age, by the way, is twenty."

Chris muttered something in a desperate, unrecognizable voice. Jess touched her husband. "At least, she's safe. She *is* safe, isn't she, Bick?"

"Sure," Bick said too quickly. "Sure. It's just a matter of getting her and the Alvaros out of that farmhouse without massacring a bunch of half-baked kids who are being used, and ruthlessly exploited, but not by Alvaro's people. They don't know any more than we do about it. Someone else is using them . . . I wish I knew who."

"But what is it to them, these kids, I mean?" Chris asked understanding nothing.

Jessica stared so hard at the distant, shadowed farmhouse it was as if she could see her child there, a pawn to win recognition of a union, a preposterous and impossible blackmail attempt. It was so preposterous that once again she began to suspect there was a great deal more to it than an attempt to help a civil rights movement.

"Bick! Does anyone know any more about how the attack on Alvaro himself is to take place? There is one, you know. Every member of the grape-growers seems to know about it."

"Nothing definite. Every single man, woman, and child over there between those trucks and trailers has been searched and double-searched. A few shivs, a busted shotgun, that's all. All the cars, trucks, trailers, everything's been gone through. X-ray eyes. Nothing missed. If someone has hired one of those poor devils to kill his leader, it isn't anyone who's there now."

"Probably one of the sweet, innocent kids lying in wait out there in those fields," Chris put in. "Can't we just drive over them to the farmhouse? I don't mean literally, but — just force our way? If they want to get their heads knocked, that's their problem. I want my daughter back, and I want her *now!*"

"I know. I intend to get Bethy. If that posse and those kids just give me ten minutes alone."

The sheriff's posse, having marched unimpeded through the workers' camp, was already spread out along the field and moving forward. One of the staring dark-faced laborers cried suddenly, "They do no harm, señor. They no hurt the little señorita. They are for Alvaro. They only try to help us, those children, is all." But nobody in authority heard him.

Bick moved away from the Marches abruptly. "I've got to get there. Maybe I can make it before the riot starts. You two stay here, behind the car. I hope to God that trigger-happy sheriff doesn't start shooting."

Chris said angrily, "I'm going along. Show me what to do. God! I wish I had a gun."

Jess and Bick exchanged quick glances, and the latter muttered, "Just what we need about now!"

Sirens blasted the night as more official cars drove up, coming to a stop in a cloud of dust that almost engulfed the Marches. Chris got Jessica out of their way, and when they recovered they found Bick several yards off, his dark shirt and dungarees helping him to dissolve into the starless dark. Chris started after him, but a voice called from among the men with badges, "They're coming out — the Alvaros. Don't nobody do nothing."

Jessica caught Chris's arm. "Can you see them? Is Bethy with them?" Together they began to run through a deep, dry furrow just beyond the pool of light from the temporary generators. They could see only two people, a man and a woman . . . the Alvaros. They walked slowly over the wagon road that curved along the furrows from the farmhouse to the crowded highway. They would have to pass the farm-workers' camp, but Jess was not afraid for them there. It was the long walk past unseen bodies, all those hidden twenty-year-olds who either were or only pretended to be hippies and supporters from the state's universities.

Heads rose everywhere out of the dark fields, all looking young and unkempt, and, in any other circumstance, would have been ridiculous to Jess. Tonight she suspected them of any possible crime. Her head ached, and she called out to Chris, "Wait! Please wait!"

Chris had just turned and was reaching out his hand to her when, a hundred yards across the field behind him, she saw a faint flicker of a light against the twilight darkness. It took her only a second or two to realize that it might very likely be a rifle barrel, and if so, the Alvaros were in the direct line of fire. Jess whispered, "Those kids aren't supposed to be armed! They're supposed to be putting up passive resistance, to protect Alvaro and the migrants."

Before Chris could make out the thing she saw, two loud shots exploded from another direction entirely, near the sheriff's advancing line of men. They met their first resistance and scuffles had begun. Like everyone else, Chris was looking toward the posse, but Jess, though startled, had noted a movement from the field — the light on that mysterious rifle barrel. She screamed, piercing, ear-splitting sounds, and a second later two things happened: the Alvaros fell flat to the ground, and two shots were fired from that hidden rifle barrel. The sounds had almost, but not quite been muffled by the sound of the first shots, ostensibly fired by the sheriff's posse.

After that, panic and confusion were everywhere across the field. The attempt to shoot the Alvaros had obviously shaken the young people. They came pouring out from every direction, complaining furiously about double-crosses and being held off from their hero, Juan Alvaro, whom Jess could see now getting to his feet and helping his wife.

"They're all right, Jess," Chris assured her. "That precious rabble-rouser will live to rouse another day. Well, we can thank God for that. Now, let's get to Bethany and that Romeo of yours."

Jess, who had thought a minute before that her heart would burst with her anguish and fear was amazed to find herself able to hobble along beside Chris through the deep, dusty furrow because at the end of that furrow she saw Bick Haldean's big form, and, more important, beside him huddled in an old leather jacket young Bethy was frightened but still game.

- SIXTEEN -

Chris stopped on the saddle of the highway before getting into the car. Jessica, who had gone on with Bethy, turned to watch him, troubled by his silence since an hour ago when he had run to meet his shivering daughter in the dusty field.

"What is it, Chris? Is everything all right?"

He moved on slowly looking puzzled and lost, all his assurance gone. "I don't understand it . . . not any of it. Those kids out there in the field were hardly older than Robin. Even the assassin didn't look much older."

"Most of them mean well," Jess consoled him because he was so disturbed. She herself had found herself disturbed for years by this phenomenon of the aware younger generation. It was perhaps good for Chris that he too had finally opened his eyes. "Anyway, it isn't your fault. Come along."

He nodded and then said something she couldn't believe she had heard: "This Alvaro seems to understand them. Maybe Bethany will tell me how he does it."

"Mom, did you hear that?" Bethy whispered. "I think he means it. Just think! Daddy's grown up!"

Jess smiled tenderly. She thought Bethy had made a profound observation about Christopher March.

The Marches, with Bethy huddled shivering between them, crowded into the back seat of Bick Haldean's car, while one of the Sacramento police who had escorted them to Bolano slid into the front seat beside Bick.

"Sorry to intrude on you folks. I know you want your privacy, but I got my orders. Got to look out for your safety, and all that."

There had been innumerable delays before they were able to leave the scene of the attempted murders. The riot which had threatened at the time the shots were fired seemed to have sputtered out, chiefly because of shock at the murder attempts. The sheriff's men steered the youngsters out of the fields, let some of them drive away, and booked the more profane members of the mob under the all-seeing eyes of Bick and other newsmen, while a representative of the local district attorney's office typed up statements on the spot for Jess to sign as an eyewitness to the actual murder shots. Two suspects were taken away, one of whom had fired the shots at Juan Alvaro while the other fired the diversionary shots near the posse in an attempt to make it appear that the killing of Alvaro was an accident at the hands of careless possemen.

"But the two killers did look just like the other college kids," Bethy objected plaintively. "Somebody says they're in their late twenties. We all thought they belonged in the student groups."

"Never mind, dear," Jess tried to soothe the girl as they drove away from the scene. "Everyone will know your friends were innocent. They meant well."

"On the other hand," Chris protested, looking over Bethy's head to his wife, "if the Alvaros hadn't walked out of the farmhouse to end the silly sit-in, you'd all still be prisoners in that place."

But Bethy had not forgotten her hero. "That was Bick who bullied those kids around the house into letting him in to get me. Of course, the Alvaros walking out like that distracted their attention. Anyway," she shivered and sighed, sinking back down between her parents, "it may all have been for the best. Nobody will dare try to murder anybody after those hoods confess."

"No," Chris agreed firmly. "And there will be no more hints to me about how they're 'getting rid of Alvaro.' I don't hold with murder."

"Glad to hear that," murmured Bick from the front seat.

The speeding car reached the March home just as the sun was rising and Bick said good night to the Marches on the steps.

"I'll do my best to keep the press away for a few hours," he told Chris, "but there's bound to be a deluge later today."

Chris nodded. The strain of the night's happenings had aged him; the hand he held out to Bick was not quite as steady as usual. "I want to thank you for getting my little girl out of there."

But Bick, having taken the offered hand, brushed aside thanks briskly: "It was all over when you people saw the shots fired. The kids meant no harm. It was their silly way of forcing a settlement. They had simply accepted the assassins in their midst the way all of us accept evil without recognizing it." He went down the steps, then turned and looked up at Jess. "I'll be over to see you late today." Then he drove off with the Sacramento officer, leaving the Marches to the attentions of a chattering, wildly excited Robin and Jessica's nurse who disapproved of the whole thing.

Strangely enough — strange to the nurse — Jessica's exertions did not seem to have bothered her. She had suffered no physical ill-effects from her violent twenty-four hours.

She was awake, dressed and downstairs before Chris himself got up. One look at the evening's edition of the influential *Oakland Tribune* made her wonder if Chris would want to get up. The headline blazed:

MARCH-ALVARO TIEUP?

The article went on to speculate that since, as the paper put it, the Marches had saved Juan Alvaro's life, a collaboration between them was being talked about in political circles. Chris would hate it, she was sure. It got worse — or better? — in the editorial.

"The old, staunchly liberal Christopher March may not be as dead as his enemies pretend."

The editorial went on to build up an even rosier picture of Chris, boy liberal, and Jess couldn't help wishing it might rub off on Chris. Behind her, Robin whistled, and she turned and offered him the paper.

"No, thanks, Mother. I saw the bad news — that is, Father's sure to call it bad news. I think it would be great, don't you?"

"Marvelous. What have you got there? Any mail for me?"

"Matter of fact, there is, Mother. It's Grandmother's writing, but the envelope says personal. Have you got secrets with Grandmother?"

She took the gold-bordered white envelope from Robin so quickly he was startled. "Hey!

That's what I call snatching it."

"Please, Robin, be quiet just for a minute." She slit open the envelope and took out the creamy double page. She read with difficulty Augusta March's characteristic scrawl:

My dear,

I realize how upset you were over our phone call last night. You must have thought the whole world was in on the simple, practical matter of getting Thea Souza's girl and my boy started in life. I was broke as usual, but I had political connections. I contributed those; Thea contributed eight thousand dollars. She didn't steal it, and she didn't mortgage the old homestead. She simply sold the A.T. & T. stock she had been adding to for your inheritance. She felt, and rightly, I think, that you children needed it more at the beginning of your married life.

My dear, do not blame that generous Thea or me. Remember instead how happy she was that she lived to see her daughter as a U.S. Congressman's wife.

Forgive me, Jessica? You will understand, I hope, that we couldn't tell you. You might have told Christopher, and he must never know.

Love, Augusta.

"What you laughing about, Mother? Let me in on it," Robin begged.

"Sorry, dear. It's one of those lovely woman-type letters."

She tore the letter into bits, still laughing, and dropped them into the ashtray where she lit them with the Op Art cigarette lighter. She had just finished burning the last bit when Robin called her into the foyer.

A noisy engine was abruptly killed in front of the house, and Jess went to the foyer window to look out at the street.

"I'll bet it's the reporters," Robin exclaimed excitedly. "They probably want an interview with Father, the new liberal."

Chris called to them from the stairs: "Not quite, I'm afraid. Jess, Haldean just called. He's on his way here. He asked me —" He glanced at wide-eyed Robin. "He said he had something to say to you. But I'd appreciate it if you could see these reporters with me first."

"Certainly." Her awareness of his need for her made the mention of Bick all the more painful. She realized that any thought of hurting Chris was painful to her.

Robin rushed to the door to usher in two men from San Francisco newspapers while an attractive, tailored, fortyish woman on the steps raised a German camera to her eye. She began to snap shots of Chris behind Robin who was acting the butler, and then of Chris with Jessica who had joined her husband.

"Please come in," Jessica said to the woman with all the graciousness she could summon up. She told Robin to see if the cook could prepare canapés. Then she watched Chris make drinks for the men and for the female photographer while she made small talk. She was sure they had come to talk about Chris March's surprising return to the principles of his early political life. This return to the man who had represented the civil rights of his constituents so long ago was all based on his experiences of one night in the San Joaquin Valley. What would happen when the truth got out, that Chris's entire connection with Alvaro and the farm-labor cause was purely accidental?

"They ought to congratulate him on his real purpose: to rescue Bethy," she murmured to the returning Robin. "When he raced through that field to rescue Bethy, he was really heroic. He hated mobs and violence and unpleasant scenes. That took courage."

"Sure," Robin agreed looking at her in surprise. "I always knew Father had guts. Didn't you?"

She wondered if she looked as ashamed as she felt at her son's reminder. Then her attention was caught by something the man from the *Chronicle* said.

"I'm afraid it wasn't exactly about your new liberalism, Mr. March. I — ah — feel like the guy that brought the bad news to the Persian Kings and got beheaded for it. You see, it just came over the wires: the president sort of let it leak out that his choice for vice-president wouldn't be anybody in his cabinet. As he puts it, 'they're all too valuable in their present jobs.' So he feels the best man for the nomination would be, say, a governor . . . preferably a governor of a Pacific Coast state — to balance the ticket."

Jessica felt Chris's fingertips touch her arm. She took his hand unobtrusively. She did not dare to look at him. She knew, from his desperately seeking hand, how much the blow had affected him. But he managed to reply with a small, though perfectly adequate laugh.

"Don't worry. I won't behead you. I've talked with the president recently. And I'm afraid I had to tell him I can do more for my constituents and my state as the senator from California than as vice-president."

They all glanced at Jess who tried not to look as startled as she felt.

But Chris had a few more words to say. "California's concerns are my concerns; we have problems, but with hard work, intelligence and understanding we can achieve much. Incidentally," he added to the scribbling reporters, "there will soon be changes in the senatorial staff. You'll be getting a formal announcement shortly."

"But Mr. March," the female photographer voiced everyone's surprise. "Is the senator — Senator Jessica . . . retiring?"

Jess had never admired her husband so much as at this worst minute of his career when he landed on his feet so brilliantly. And most important to her was that phrase about staff changes — for it meant that Chris had listened, had believed her about D.D.'s involvement in all this. There'd be no more trouble from that quarter. Jess said loudly, triumphantly, "Like my husband, I have a job I prefer. Being Christopher March's wife."

More pictures were taken this time with flash bulbs, and in the middle of the commotion, Jess turned to see Bick Haldean in the doorway. He looked as if he had heard the whole interview. She still had her hand in her husband's, and Bick saw that too. While the newsmen were discussing with Chris California's place in the next administration, and the photographer was getting out new bulbs, Bick came in and spoke to Jess in a low voice.

"Is it true?"

Feeling that she had betrayed him, she confessed, "I think it is. In a funny sort of way, we're starting again, Chris and I."

"It will end the same way, and you know it. You'll give your health, maybe your life."

"Not this time." She smiled at him gently as possible. "Now I'm grown up . . . and I know how much he needs me. It took me eighteen years to find out."

Chris looked around. The tension in his face relaxed a little. She was sure he had heard her conversation with Bick. "My ears are burning. Is somebody talking about me?" he asked lightly.

Jessica raised their clasped hands and shook them in the old, companionable way. "Yes, dear. We were. I told Bick about our future plans. Bick, thank God I'm going back to being merely Mrs. Christopher March, and Chris — well, he was always the real senator. And he's going to run in my place, this fall."

Bethy had come downstairs and run to thank Bick for what she called his gallant rescue, and she and Robin cornered Bick to get the particulars about last night's arrests. Smothered by their questions, he gradually moved away with them, explaining.

"Yes, the Clormann outfit hired the assassin and his accomplice. Of course, they're denying it, but the signed confessions . . ."

Chris and Jessica stood there, momentarily alone. He studied their clasped hands.

"Do you mind very much, coming back to me?" he asked after an uneasy silence.

"Don't be silly. We were made for each other. I need you, and you — you really do need me."

He stared at her in complete astonishment. "I've always needed you. I could never get anywhere, be anything, if you weren't with me, didn't you know that?"

She smiled, treasuring the assurance she had been seeking for so many years. "Of course, I always knew," she lied brightly.